The Hope Chest

To the Pocella's
One of the nicest familys
I know from
my family
Pat Hogeboom

The Hope Chest

P. S. Hogeboom

Copyright © 2003 by P. S. Hogeboom.

Library of Congress Number: 2003092706

ISBN :   Hardcover   1-4010-9778-2
    Softcover   1-4010-9777-4

This is a work of fiction. Names, characters, places and incidents either are the product of the author's imagination or are used fictitiously, and any resemblance to any actual persons, living or dead, events, or locales is entirely coincidental.

This book was printed in the United States of America.

To order additional copies of this book, contact:
Xlibris Corporation
1-888-795-4274
www.Xlibris.com
Orders@Xlibris.com
18129

Contents

Acknowledgements

Hazel Schrack of Elm Creek kept her journals well, and is the inspiration for this story of prairie lives in transition. For lives well and honorably lived, shared with me in friendship and inspiration, thanks go to William and Laura Schrack of Elm Creek, Nebraska, their children, Vern, Hazel, Stella, Royal, Viola, Leona and Bill and their children and grandchildren. They are all fine human beings and represent the best in American life.

Love and thanks to Nettie, Minnie, and Jeannette who set the standards high. To my own Willard, my forever thanks and enduring love.

* * *

Thanks also to Carolyn Bachsmith of *PATCHWORKS*, Sayville New York for offering me the opportunity to appreciate what quilting is all about. Her original quilt kits are available through her web site, *www.patchworks.com*.

To *Careyj@bluepoint.com:* FYI. Family Reunion just around corner. Just found old Aunt Eva's Journals. Will be reading them aloud. You can stay with us at farm. I want us to meet so much. You and me only ones close in age. Just send time and air. Will meet you. Hope u can make it. Love and stuff, cousin Sally.

To *Fishers@libsearch.org.* So look forward to meeting every one, especially you Sally. The journals sound great. My Grandfather, Papa Roy used to talk about his sister, Eva Jean, all the time. They must have been very close. Did you all know much about her? See you Omaha @ 10:30am. on Friday. USAir. Thanks again. Cousin Jeannie.

To *Careyj@bluepoint.com:* Woopee! See ya 10:30. We all knew Aunt Eva. Did you know she lived to be 100?

Chapter One

Cousin Jeannie

An exhausted Jeannie Carey settled into the seat and tried to distract herself by looking out the plane window but saw instead her own eyes reflected back at her—the sadness, the tension in her once vibrant features, the worry lines over her eyes.

To herself she said, "This is the right thing to do. Got to get out of here. See new people. This is a good thing. Meet my family. I'm not alone. I have family."

But she saw her face once more, and wondered,

"Will I ever be pretty again?"

For a moment she buried her face in her hands and rubbed her temples, then shook her head and tried to relax.

The breakup with Brad had been devastating. For months she had cried when she was alone, had laughed too loud with others, and the depression that followed the end of their relationship had been debilitating. She couldn't eat or sleep.

"But I'm finally stick thin." She thought. "Every girl's dream!" The face in the window stared back at her, the lips curved in a rueful smile.

It had gone too far. Jeannie looked wan and worn out. When her cousin had notified her about the reunion, she knew at once that she would go. Papa Roy had been the first man in her life that Jeannie knew consciously she loved. She smiled when she thought of him. Oh, she'd loved her Daddy too, very much, but it was Papa Roy who was around when she was really small. Her Daddy was off making a living then and didn't have much time for her. Papa Roy did and he just adored his little granddaughter. Family had been so important to him. Jeannie suddenly realized that she hadn't thought of that for years. Papa Roy had always talked about family and how much you could count on them. How had she managed to forget it? She was glad to remember it now. Of course with Brad there was never time to think of anything like this. If they were still together she would not be going out West now, she knew that.

Sally's e-mail had come at just the right time. Jeannie wanted to go—to get away, to do something totally different, so she'd reached for the phone and made her reservations in the next few minutes before she'd even tried to convinced her boss she'd need the time; that it was important to do this "family" thing. They were glad to give her the time off. Jeannie was one of their stars.

One of the problems Jeannie was having in midst of this depression was that she couldn't stick to a decision. She would second-guess herself with every one she made and this was no exception. Then she just decided to do it, not think about it, and the next thing she knew it was time to go.

"Daddy would be pleased too." Jeanne thought. "I'm going for him. If he were alive he'd be there. He must have known her—this Aunt Eva person. OK. I'm going for Daddy, and for Papa Roy—not for me because I am now a nut, but for them."

Quietly, Jeannie smiled. She didn't know that her own lovely, warm smile returned as she thought of them both, Father— Grandfather. Sighing, she finally relaxed.

She promised herself she'd see a shrink when she got back to New York. Maybe that would do something for her and help to get her past this whole thing. She'd lost a boyfriend, not her life. She was grieving too much and she somehow knew she needed help to move on.

"How will I know her?" Jeanne thought as she walked along the portal, her bag rolling behind her.

There was no mistaking Sally. There she was in jeans and curly long hair, grinning ear to ear and jumping up and down.

"Jeannie, over here. Howdy!"

Before Jeannie had a second to react to the unfamiliar greeting, the soft twang, she was wrapped in Sally's arms. Her New York reserve was startled, but Sally didn't seem to notice. They both laughed. And then laughed again as they saw how much alike they were. They were the same height, and their hair curled and was parted on the same side. Sally's was longer, lighter, streaked with the sun. Jeannie's was streaked too, expensively, from a bottle and her cut was fashion's latest. But it was their smile that was almost exactly the same, wide and even, it crinkled their eyes and showed their almost matching cheekbones.

"Oh, we're so glad you could come. This is so great. At last a great excuse to finally meet, huh? This is my husband Virgil. Here honey, take her bags" which he was already doing.

He smiled and nodded a shy "Howdy" too, and in only a few seconds they were on their way.

Jeannie had landed in Omaha dressed in her classy business suit from DKNY, with her oh-so-perfect hair-do, not too groomed, not too casual and the just right pin on her lapel, perfect pumps, not too clunky, definitely not dainty. She screamed New York City and she knew it the minute she got off the plane and noticed that about 90% of the people in the airport were wearing jeans.

Jeannie found herself babbling.

"I can't wait to get out of these clothes, Sally. God, it's great to meet you. Where are we going? I hope I'm not in the way. I just wanted to be here. Chance to meet the family, you know, and my Dad and Papa Roy would want me to come."

"We thought it was so nice that you called your Grandad, "Papa Roy." They've carried the name Royal on for two generations now. Time for another one. I remember your Grandfather from when Great Aunt Leona died. Such a nice man."

"I hope it's OK that I'm here. I really don't know anybody."

It had been more than OK. All the Aunts and cousins, both first and second and a few once—removed, seemed genuinely thrilled that she'd taken the time from her big city life to come. They had greeted her warmly and put her to work setting the big table at first—cousin Kay's house for the mounds of food that would follow the get together.

By the time the first evening was over Jeannie was completely at ease with Sally. This country cousin was very special. Sally worked hard on the farm helping her husband and raising their three kids. She was a farm wife who spent many hours in the sun and the wind. No fancy beauty shops for Sally. Jeannie noticed how pampered her own hands with her long acrylic nails looked next to this cousin whose unvarnished nails were clean and clear.

She had packed so fast that Jeannie hadn't had any time to think about how she'd look in her New York clothes. She threw in some leggings and tunics and boots, a plain skirt, and a change of tops to wear with the black suit she arrived in. It was conservative, simple, and for this place—all wrong. She didn't own a pair of jeans any more. Since the break up with Brad, Jean had thrown away all the country clothes she had worn when she'd weekended with him at the country home he'd bought outside of Poughkeepsie. It was an old farmhouse in terrible shape but on a nice piece of land. She had done all the redecorating herself, sure that one day it would be her home too. She loved the countryside and looked forward to spending long, lovely weekends there. Which did she feel worse about, losing him, or losing the house?

She was keenly aware of how different she must seem to them in leggings and tunics. The skirt she'd arrived in was so short she'd seen the men's eyes blink when they first saw her. Then there was Sally, no make up, in jeans and a sweater looking fabulous and right.

Late that night, tucked into the old bedstead at the farm, Jeannie found herself so comfortable that she was ready to fall asleep almost at once.

"There's a whole world outside of New York, where a life can be lived without being scared. I think I like this—" and before the thought could be finished she was asleep.

The reunion itself was such good fun. Jeannie met more cousins, old ones and young ones and there was no way she could keep them all apart. They dined together at a restaurant where they had Buffalo steaks, barbequed beans and three different kinds of pie. For the first time in months, Jeannie enjoyed every bite of her food.

Sally read aloud pages from a favored ancestor, Papa Roy's sister just passed at almost 100 years old. Her journals dated from 1912. They all laughed at some of the archaic language. She called her students, "scholars" and her stories of teaching on the prairie when she just a girl herself were wonderful to hear. Sally was a librarian and she was the one who set up the children's book readings, so she was a good reader and did the journals justice.

The family—she thought of them as family now—spoke of Aunt Eva Jeannette Carey with great affection. It was clear that she was very respected, and certainly much loved by them all. They spoke of her education. She was the first person in the family, man or woman, to go to college and get a degree, then a Master's. She was the first of many teachers in the family. She had helped to educate her nieces and nephews and then had helped the next generation too.

"Very nice indeed." Jeannie said, but in truth it was all so far away from her own life and times that she couldn't really relate.

It was this new family who impressed her the most. She loved the sound of Nebraska in their speech, and their attitude toward life. Naively, she'd asked about the size of the farms they owned. She was amazed that she had family who owned hundreds of acres of land.

She had charmed them when she'd said, "Wow, most people I know think they're really something if they've got two bedrooms!"

They laughed a lot, and Jeannie did too, listening as they

told stories on one another, and shared a comfortable easy camaraderie of family and familiarity. Jeannie didn't quite know what to make of it. Nobody she knew; nothing she had ever experienced was quite like this. She relaxed and spent time listening, comfortable with these decent people. They were friendly, kind and accepting. Nothing like the pressured, analyzing, stressed people in her world. It was a relief, a respite in fact.

Then there was Sally—what to make of Sally.

Here was a girl who could be her twin, happily married to Virgil Fisher, a nice, friendly guy. She worked her butt off on a farm where she cooked, cleaned, mucked, hand-painted barns and then sat back every night on the swing on the porch with her husband by her side, looking up at stars. They had invited her to join them on her last night. Jeannie was awed by it. She'd never seen a sky like that in her life. She watched Sally and Virgil sit side-by-side, almost cuddling, but holding back a bit. They giggled quietly and gazed at one another as they all sat chatting. Somehow, Jeannie knew that if she hadn't been there, Sally would have had her head on Virgil's shoulder.

As if Sally didn't work hard enough on the farm, she also worked at the library 20 hours a week. It was a forty-five minute drive to get there, but with everything else she had to do she seemed to love working with books and with people. That wasn't all. She'd also started a reading group for little kids, and was studying the computer by teaching herself from books. She'd even set up the library's e-mail which was how she had contacted Jeannie.

Suddenly it was over. Sally drove her back to Omaha for the plane and this time they had both hugged as they'd said goodbye. "Wouldn't you like to visit NYC", Jeannie had blurted. "I'd love to have you. Come any time."

But soon, as she sat back in her seat on the plane she felt like such a hypocrite.

"What was I thinking—making such a stupid offer?" She thought. "What on earth would I do with her in New York? I have to work. She'd be lost without a guide. "Damn!"

She knew she'd just been swept away by the genuineness of her country cousins. They wouldn't make an offer they didn't mean. The closer she got to New York, the more the pain came back.

Suddenly she felt the tears again too, hurting just behind her eyes. Yes, wasn't it nice that this ancient aunt of hers had such a good life. She'd been married too, something Jeannie now doubted she would ever have.

She thought to herself. "She was probably married at 15 or something."

Jeanne sighed and reached for the box with the funny old booklets that her cousin had given her just before she got on the plane.

"We talked about it," Sally had said, "and thought that you should read these. They're all of Aunt Eva's journals. There are letters too, and some other stuff. She kept them all these years, and they were close to her when she died. She never gave them away like she did most of her things. But we don't want them to be lost and we don't know what to do with them. So we thought you should have them. To tell you the truth Jeannie, we sort of hope you'll know someone in New York who'll be interested in them. There's a wonderful story here and it would make a great book. So—take care of them will you?"

Jeannie was stunned by the trust in this gift. She knew it wasn't easy to let the fragile books go. They trusted her and they hardly knew her. She had tears in her eyes when she held them to her breast and accepted the little booklets all wrapped up to keep them safe.

"I—I don't know what to say. Thank you. I'll take good care of them for my Dad and my Grandpa too. Tell them all won't you. You'll hear from me. I'll keep them safe."

Sally saw that Jeannie was truly moved and she relaxed. It had been hard to give up the journals, but she had a good feeling now that they were doing the right thing.

"She was quite a gal, Aunt Eva, and you didn't have a chance to know her. We'd like to know that if you don't know what to do with them, you'll send them back to us. We think that we'd put them in the library at the University."

In answer, Jeannie just leaned forward and kissed her cousin. She patted the books and held them close without another word. Sally knew they were safe.

Now, comfortably seated on the plane, Jeannie opened the box and found some books wrapped in tissue paper and then in an old fabric. There were letters too, all carefully kept in the original envelopes. She had never seen anything quite like the journals. They were soft-covered, brown, **I Am It** journals with red binding and as she opened them, she realized that they were terribly old, and somewhat fragile, but the thread binding still held strong as she turned the pages and started to read.

October 20, 1912: I am eighteen years old today, my most special birthday ever. A-pink-birthday-cake-day. And the sun knew it too, because it shined so fine it made everything all pink. Mr. Johannson gave me a special gift I'll wear forever, and Royal came too. Royal gave me this very journal to write in, and I wonder if someone else might read it someday. Uncle Elroy and Aunt Stella made me the best birthday present any girl ever had. I want to remember this day forever.

Chapter Two

The Pink-Birthday-Cake-Day

The window in the little wooden house was dirty as it always was from the prairie winds, but Eva Jean's heart was so happy that she leaned against that old window and beamed her special smile as if she were looking at a rose garden—her dream rose garden—instead of at the gray and solemn sky. She was dreaming. Dreaming of her future with Mr. Johannson, Thomas, her gentleman, her sweetheart. At the thought her face colored.

"My sweetheart! He's my own, my sweetheart!" And the words thrilled her.

Her hands held the piece-work she always had close to her, something that she was making by hand. It might be a gift for someone, or perhaps, more practically, some part of her own wardrobe—a blouse for instance, only she called it a "waist".

Eva Jean's hands were seldom still, and she was never far from her piece—work bag full of cloth. She hoarded cloth like gold. She went through the leftovers from the church rummage for the poor and found bits of dresses and skirts sometimes with just a small piece worth saving. Then she'd wash and cut them carefully, separating them by colors.

Aunt Stella helped her gather the prints, saving old clothes and letting her cut up aprons before they were fully worn out, which was quite an extravagance on the prairie where people held on to things until they were worn out, but Eva Jean was so good with her quilts, that she wanted to encourage her.

This time her hands held a square of quilting, or an almost square of pieces that she would sew together all by herself, one square at a time, to make a quilt. It was her future she held in her hands; the first part of the quilt that would cover her and Thomas someday, when they were—could she say the words—"man and wife". Oh, as she thought the very words, her heart danced and so did her feet and she whirled away from that dingy old window and spun around the little room. The quilt pieces went flying as she did and the colors for the old fashioned Irish Chain pattern flashed in the air.

"Well now Missy! What's this?"

The door banged behind her as Aunt Stella came into the room. Booted and jacketed against the wind, she carried a bag of potatoes from the storm cellar.

'Looks like a lot of silliness, girl. You should be getting ready for school."

Eva Jean knew she was right. She should be planning her next day's work for her scholars at the town school.

"Oh Auntie I can't help it. It's just such a wonderful day!" She scurried then, to gather all her pieces once more, while Aunt Stella shook her head, a tiny smile playing at her lips. She dropped the heavy bag and stood with her hands on her hips.

"Wonderful? What are you looking at? It's same as it's been all day, just awful!"

"Yes, but I started my very own quilt, and the sun will come out you'll see, and I'm a teacher, and I'm going to have my own money, and someday, I'll have a home and a family. It's a wonderful day, Auntie. Wonderful!"

"Right glad you think so, How about helping us to have a wonderful meal anyway!"

But Eva was too happy to start peeling potatoes just yet.

"I will. Back in a minute." and before Stella could protest, she was wrapped in the old shawl that hung near the door and was out the door, just as the sun came peeping under the clouds.

Aunt Stella just shook her head as Eva Jean danced out the door.

"My, my what a change from our too tired teacher!"

She was right. Eva Jean's day had begun at 5:00 as she had risen, helped with the breakfast for the hands, walked in the dark to the school, started the coal stove, managed her students all day, then walked the two miles back home. As usual, she was almost white with exhaustion when she had walked in the door.

Aunt Stella chuckled as she set up the potatoes, pumped some water up at the sink and settled into peeling them.

"This boy had better be some fine fellow for our girl." she thought. "Hope they don't jump into anything too fast. Eva Jean's got a future of her own. Doesn't have to be a farm wife."

She sighed, thinking of the hard days that were all she knew, and her own baby girl buried in the yard out back. Eva Jean had been with them since her parents had both died of smallpox when she and her brother Royal were 7. Stella and Elroy had tried to raise them both for several years, but then Royal went to live with the oldest married sister. It was Eva Jean who was like their own.

Uncle Elroy found her there, sitting real quiet like. He knew she was worried about something and his hand went gently to her shoulder. She reached up and patted it.

"It's all right, Elroy. Just worried about Eva Jean and this boy. They seem so young."

"Why Stella Schrack, you were 17 when we got hitched."

"I know. But she's got a real job and she's good at it. Hate to see her always have to work as hard as us."

"Well, now, Let's just see what this evening brings. Don't you worry. Here, let me help with that." And the two of them stood side by side, peeling a whole bucket of potatoes.

Outside, Eva Jean was still in her impossibly happy mood, all her tiredness gone. Suddenly the day was changed altogether. The heavy clouds that she had watched as the rain crossed the prairie from the West were tinged with pink as the sun made ready to set.

"This must be the color of a real sea shell," thought Eva Jean. "It's so delicate, so fragile."

She had only read about sea shells as she'd never been more than 10 miles away from home in the very middle of Nebraska in her whole life. The only body of water she knew was the Platte River, running to overflowing in the spring, but a dry and disappearing mud flat later on in the year.

The light was fragile. Any minute the color could fade to gray again. But no, this day it didn't fade, and as Eva Jean watched, the pinkness spread from cloud to cloud, and then touched the very earth with the glow of the late setting sun and she made a vow.

"I'll never forget this day. It's a pink-birthday-cake day. Yes, it is. It's just like the prettiest birthday cake that a girl could ever have." She felt giddy as the sun itself was seen at the very edge of the farthest cloud, some 60 miles away across the flat lands of Nebraska. It was a strange feeling for a girl whose life was so serious, joy, rare. But it was such a good feeling; to have hope for the future—to have a love all her own.

Eva Jean faced the sun and let it bathe her face with its pink light. She closed her eyes and memorized the feeling of it warming her skin though the air was cold. The smile had never left her face.

She was almost delirious with joy. Mr. Johannson had asked her to have an "understanding" on this very day, her 18th birthday, October 20th 1912. She had said, yes she would. She'd agreed to wait for him while he traveled to make his fortune, which would someday be their fortune. She agreed to write to him as he sent his address from far away places. She'd agreed to be true to him, which meant that she would not walk through the town with any other gentleman. She would not go with their group of friends to the next town in the horse and buggy to dances or church socials. She would keep herself just for him. And she was thrilled to say yes. It was what she had dreamed of for at least a year now.

Tonight he would come for dinner to celebrate her birthday, and he would tell Aunt Stella and Uncle Elroy. He didn't need to ask her hand so formally—not just yet, particularly since she had no mother and father living to ask, but he thought it only right that they announce their "someday intentions"

She was to have her birthday cake that night at the simple table, but her cake was hardly like the pink dream cake made from the light of the sun and clouds. It was a sturdy fruit cake made from Aunt Stella's dried fruits. Dark and solid, it would be delicious served with fresh cream so thick it didn't have to be whipped. Stella even had a small candle on it as a special treat.

In honor of the occasion, Thomas was dressed in a clean shirt and wore suspenders with his wool trousers. He looked so neat and polished that Eva Jean had giggled when she opened the door to him. Much too shy to even think of stealing a kiss, they both reached out to each other and held hands briefly and looked into each other's eyes before she welcomed him into the simple farmhouse.

Thomas was a fine looking boy. He was a rare sight in these parts with hair that was light; his Scandinavian roots no doubt. His smile was broad, when he did smile which was not often. He was a serious sort, but his features were more relaxed whenever he was with Eva Jean, and the smile was welcome. Eva Jean was tiny, only 5'1, and Thomas, at 5'7" was perfect next to her. The whole town buzzed with what a pretty couple they made.

The house was fragrant with the supper Aunt Stella had prepared. The roasting pork with rosemary from her late summer garden mingled its scent with the dinner rolls that were her specialty. Stella was a wonderful baker. Her breads and rolls were so good she often baked extra to sell at Arnott's General for a Saturday. Served with the jams Stella and Eva Jean had made in August, the pickled beets put up in September, the carrots, buttered and caramelized and the potatoes whipped with a special turn by Uncle Elroy, it was a feast.

At dinner they spoke of Thomas' plans to try to get work as a salesman. He thought that he could be good at it.

"I like people and I've never been shy of working hard. Now that I have Eva Jean to think of, I'll be wanting to work even harder."

Eva Jean smiled with such joy that Aunt Stella shook her head in amusement.

"Eva Jean says you're going to go away from us. I thought you wanted to farm, Tom?" Uncle Elroy asked.

Well, yes sir, I do, but I need to earn some money first. They talk of opening up some land over West and then I'll be ready. We'll homestead there. But I'm going to Lincoln to work first."

None of them noticed Stella's face at the mention of the word, "homestead."

Uncle Elroy's great bushy eyebrows came together.

"Lincoln!" Hmm! What're you going to do there? Do you have any prospects Tom?"

"Yes, sir. There's a friend I know who knows someone who is selling these cars. He promised to get me a meeting with the boss."

"Cars!" Filthy things will change the country. Noisy too. Won't have much peace. Just hope they don't come whizzing through here. You got a big market for em'? How can you make much money?"

"Well sir, I got to look things over and see the way the wind blows. But I do know farm machinery and there is a market there for sure. So if the car business don't work out, I'll look into farm machinery. I'll be OK. You're right about cars though. They will change things pretty good."

"Yeah, they'll change things all right, but I don't know if it'll be pretty or it'll be good."

Uncle Elroy chuckled at his own cleverness.

Dinner was about over and suddenly there was a knock at the door. "Well now, who on earth—?"

Aunt Stella rose to open the door, but Uncle Elroy stopped her.

"Just let me see who this is, at this time of night, Stel. Don't want to invite in trouble."

He walked to the door and opened it a crack then threw it opened as he called.

"Royal, my boy! Look who's here! It's your brother, Eva Jean."

At his name Eva Jean's face lit up like a lamp on a dark night. She was at the door in a moment and this time, nothing held her affection back as she threw herself into her brother's arms and hugged him.

"Oh My Gosh! How'd ya' get here? Where'd ya' come from? Come on in. Oh, I'm so glad you're here."

He was a handsome boy. His light brown hair was tousled from the wind, and his checks ruddy. His hazel eyes almost disappeared in the grin of his affectionate greeting to his favorite sister. They had been the closest in a family of seven children, coming, to his mother's embarrassment, only 10 months apart. He'd been crazy about his baby sister from the beginning and they had always been close. They had even developed their own personal language when they were very small and sometimes strangers had thought they were twins.

"Well, it took a while but I came on the 6:13. Sammy let me hitch a ride when they stopped. Walked to Kearney and the wind slowed me down a bit. But I made it! Couldn't miss your birthday, Eva Jeannette." Royal was just about the only one who called her by her full name. It was a mouthful for most people, but he knew she was named for their mother and Grandmother and it was an honor to those now dead relatives, to speak the whole name together—at least once in awhile.

"Missed you Royal. I'm so glad you're here. You remember Mr. Johannson?"

"Tom, sure do, Glad to see you. You keeping my sister busy are you?" he said with a wink, and Eva Jean gave him a look.

She also moved closer to Thomas and linked her arm in his.

"Oh, ho! So that's the way it is? Well now, tell me sir. Are your intentions honorable?"

He was laughing and his eyes twinkled as he put Mr. Johannson on the spot.

For a minute, Thomas was put off, but then he realized he was being ribbed and smiled slightly as he said.

"Yes Siree. Very honorable Sir. I hope to marry your sister some day, Sir. Do I have your permission?"

Now that really was a joke—asking her 19 year-old brother. After all, Mr. Johannson was as old as Royal, and as far as he knew Royal didn't have much in the way of prospects himself. People said he was a dreamer and a tinkerer, building silly looking crystal sets that only brought in a lot of static and didn't have much to do with anything of value. Royal had better get cracking if he was to ever have a future for himself, or so Mr. Johannson thought to himself. Still he envied the closeness this young man had to his sister. And in a fleeting thought he wondered if she would ever throw herself in his arms as she had her own brother.

Royal had brought her presents from her married sisters, of yarn for her precious handwork, and delicate batiste ordered through the Sears' catalogue. He also brought her a paper of pins and a large roll of delicate white ribbon edged in satin. Royal's gift was a journal; a group of small notebooks that said I AM IT, and a pen and ink. He knew how much she loved to write. Thomas gave her an enameled pin. It was real gold-filled, but he couldn't afford much and the pin was a very small love knot with tiny enamel work in the center. It would look pretty on all the dresses that Eva would pin it on from that day on. In fact, she would wear it so often that the enamel would wear down till it could hardly be seen. She had never had anything that was real nice, so her present thrilled her greatly.

"Well now, our gift isn't quite so fine, Eva Jean," Uncle Elroy said. "But your Aunt and me, well, we both worked on it. It's for you and this future you're planning. Put your coat on to go out back."

Aunt Stella looked pleased with him, and they all bustled out to the back of the house where there, under an old rug, was her gift.

"Your Aunt said that a modern girl needs one of these to hold all the stuff she gets together for her future."

Eva Jean knew exactly what it was.

"Oh, Uncle Elroy, you didn't. You got me a hope chest?"

"Nope—we MADE you a hope chest." And he flung back the rug to show the lovely cedar chest. Plain and simple, it nevertheless was beautifully made.

"Didn't want it to look too plain my girl, so I was able to get some good plans and make some fancy feet for the thing. Came out right nice I think." It had simply curved, sturdy feet that raised it up about six inches from the floor. It had good solid dimensions and a hand rubbed finish that glowed.

"It's so big!" I'll have a grand time filling it up! Oh, this is wonderful. Thank you all so much. You're so good to me." And she had a tear in her eye.

"Aw jeez Eva Jean. Don't you start to cry now."

"Now Royal, you watch your language, you hear." Aunt Stella scolded him gently.

"Sorry Ma'am."

"That word sounds too much like our Lord's name for decent folks to use, Roy. Don't appreciate hearing it in my house."

"Yes, Ma'am. Sorry."

Uncle Elroy gave him an affectionate and supportive pat on the shoulder. They both knew that Stella's moral code was strict, and they both abided by it.

Together the men moved the chest, hidden for some days where Eva Jean wouldn't find it, into the warm room. She was ecstatic over it and she rushed to get her quilt pieces together and place them lovingly inside. "Everything in it will be hand made. I'll be the envy of all the girls in town, Uncle." They all admired the craftsmanship in the chest. One more cup of coffee and the two young men left. They walked together to the railroad station where, with the help of his friend, Royal hopped on the train once more, lifted his cap to Thomas once and disappeared inside a railroad car.

It would be a late night for Stella and Elroy.

"Now girl you go on up and write some nice things in your journal. Elroy and I will clean up. I got plenty of biscuits left over for morning-cake too. Go on now."

"Feel better Stel? Doesn't look like they'll be making plans any time soon."

"Well he sure lights up her face. Seems like a nice boy. Hard working. But he wants to homestead! That's the hardest life there is Elroy. Let's hope he makes a go of it in Lincoln. Maybe he'll give up that idea. Just want something easier for her Elroy. Don't you see?"

He did see. He wanted Eva Jean to have a good life. One better than their own, like the life they would have wanted for their own baby girl, if she had lived. And he too had worried at the talk of homesteading. There wasn't a harder life on this earth than bending land to your own will. Man or woman, it was the hardest challenge in the west.

Eva Jean could hardly see as the tiredness seeped into her body. But she wrote in her journal and then drew a little picture of her new pin; the love knot. She added her initials entwined with Mr. Johannson's in a pretty scroll.

She was barely awake as she thanked God for his loving kindness and asked a special prayer for Royal to get back home safely. She knew that sometimes, when his friends weren't running the trains, and willing to let him on for a few miles, he would hold onto the ladder on the side of a box car. It was dangerous, and every so often someone was killed. She tried to stay awake as she prayed for her sweet Thomas, the lover with whom she had only held hands, and kissed on the cheek, and for Uncle Elroy and Aunt Stella who had spent hours, building, sanding and finishing her precious hope chest. Her last thought was of the light of the day—the Pink-Birthday-Cake Day, she knew she'd see again.

Chapter Three

Best Friends

October 24, 1912

Finished up my hanky today using a nice piece of linen and fine silk thread. It worked up just fine. Haven't done crochet lace for a long time, since Mother taught me when I was a little one. I did it double row round, but instead of putting it in my new hope chest I think I'll give it for a gift—Willa Mae, I think, would like it fine. She likes nice things. Time to think of someone else for a change since I will now spend most of my handy work time on my quilt, I am such a lucky girl. Got to say goodnight now.

The pin was secured at her neckline as Eva Jean started her work at 5:00a.m, walking to the schoolhouse as she always did. She wanted to warm it up for the children, so she always got there an hour early to set the fire, shake down the stove and put the tasks for the day on the chalkboard. It had been another windy day and the walk across the little town was lonely as usual. She didn't mind the walk even though she left so much earlier than she had as a scholar. The old kerosene lamp lit the way and she welcomed the glow it gave 'round her particularly on a bitter cold morning when the temperature dipped below 0 degrees. Her coat was as warm as a coat could be, with Aunt Stella's hand-knitted heavy shawl for added warmth, her head wrapped in another scarf and her hands in two pairs of mittens.

By the time her scholars arrived, the place was somewhat warm and as cheerful as she could make it. They arrived wearing warm, sensible clothes, carrying their books, and something in a tin for lunch. They either walked or rode a horse that they sent back home with a slap on the rear, or maybe they were driven in a wagon. Everyday they all ate together while Eva Jean helped some of them with their homework. She didn't give herself much of a break unless she had to use the privy out back. She hated it. It wasn't kept very nice; no soft paper, just old magazines for cleaning up, and if the town didn't lime it down, it got pretty rank after a few months. She made sure the children washed their hands at the wash—stand outside after they went to the privy even if they had to break ice first.

Eva Jean got the job in her own hometown because she had just graduated in June with the highest grades. There had been a graduating class of four, including her best friend, Willa Mae.

Eva Jean and Willa Mae had both gone all through school together. In fact, they had always known one another. Eva wondered sometimes if they were really best friends, or was it just that they were the only two girls the same age in the whole town, so they had to be friends. They didn't have much choice. But she didn't think about it too much. Eva Jean was like that. She accepted life as it came. Willa Mae was there. She was as familiar as the fields that Uncle Elroy farmed.

The fact that Willa Mae was the real pretty one, was not questioned. Daughter of the only man in the county of substantial means, she always had the newest and prettiest clothes. She had shiny, black hair, blue, sparkly eyes, and a dimply smile. She was soft and round and daintily plump, and she had a little girlish voice that called attention wherever she went. Eva Jean found out when they were quite young and they went with the adults to town for shopping, that it was Willa Mae who got the most attention.

She would laugh and giggle, and glance at the boys in a quick side-long glance, and they would come over and talk to her while Eva Jean stayed in the background. Not that Eva Jean wasn't also nice looking. She was. Real nice. All the ladies said she had the prettiest hair of any of the girls, soft and light brown, with waves curling around her cheeks. Her figure was slim, her eyes sparkling and her face softened with a sweet smile. But Willa, it was generally agreed, had the most delicate skin, the roundest figure shown off by the prettiest clothes. She actually washed her hair twice a week, an unheard of luxury at a time when once a month was more the custom. Of course, Eva Jean had to wash her own once a week or her curls were impossible to control.

Eventually, Miss Willa Mae Arnott would toss her head and indicate that she didn't care much what the boys thought— about anything. She was soon off to shop for something pretty for herself. The boys were left with the quiet one. Eva Jean was a good listener and she liked to hear about people and places, so the boys would tell her about their farms, and about the new magazines they were reading from the big cities and about how they hoped to get away to the big city someday. She gave them each her undivided attention and always remembered what they had said.

It was on one of those trips, when she and Willa Mae were just 16, that Eva Jean had met Mr. Johannson. He had grown up two towns away. They had probably met as children somewhere at a church social, or perhaps had just passed as their parents shopped and held their little hands as they pulled them along, in and out of stores to gather goods to take back home. Then, suddenly they didn't need to be with the grown ones anymore, so they were able to stay on the street and visit and play.

The years passed and one day, there he was.

And as usual, it was Willa Mae he started to talk to first.

"I've seen you here before haven't I?" He'd asked.

"Don't think so." she'd replied.

He was puzzled. "Don't you come regular like?"

"Why no." Willa teased. "No, I don't. Or maybe I do. But if I do you would remember me don't you think? You wouldn't have to ask."

"Well now, I just didn't notice you before, I guess." Mr. Johannson said.

"Huh!" Willa said with a toss of her head. "Well, there's no point in noticing now." And she had taken the arm of one of the other boys.

"Buy me some licorice, Mr. Smithy, will you?" And glancing over her shoulder, she waltzed away, turning her gaze on the lucky Mr. Smithy.

When he turned around, completely bewildered by that blue—eyed Miss he now knew he must have seen a hundred times, there was Eva Jean, her shy smile turning into a laugh as she said,

"Well Sir. You handled that well. We have met before, on this very street I think. You're from Kearney aren't you? I think you know my brother Royal."

"Royal Carey? Why, sure I do. That's your brother? We worked in the fields together last summer. Are you Eva Jeannette? "

Eva turned pink. "Why yes. How did you remember my name?"

"I thought it was a real different name, like Royal's as a matter of fact." Thomas was pleased to see this smiling pretty girl who certainly didn't have any airs like the other one. He felt the coins jingling in his pocket.

"Miss Carey, would you like to take a walk with me? We could stop by the general store and I'd like to buy you a soda, if that's all right with you."

He offered his arm. Eva Jean took it, still pink-cheeked, and as they walked she listened to his small talk, nodded sweetly, and looked up at him several times to try to remember him as he must have been just the year before. Just before they got to the store he turned and said. "Well now, am I handling this all right?"

And that was the beginning of it all. In no time at all, Mr. Thomas Johannson was turning up at church socials at the Methodist in Elm Creek, and was seen with other young men from the town. He'd always manage to find her, and she always was willing to walk the rails with him as they followed the train tracks. She would listen to him as he spun out his hopes and dreams to one day have a farm and land of his very own, and manage the soil as his family had done for several generations.

Mrs. Arnott said, "Willa Mae, your friend Eva Jean is such a nice girl, and she has such a nice young man. And she's smart too, to be asked to teach. I wish it had been you, but of course, you never liked learning all that much. What's the matter with you? Why haven't you found a nice fellow yet? Well never mind, I know you'll meet someone as soon as you can."

Miss Willa Mae Arnot was furious. She should be the first to have a beau. She should be the one to have the town smiling about the walks and the shyness of two young people together. Willa Mae was mad and she was wildly jealous of Eva Jean who didn't guess a thing. In fact, Eva Jean was so trusting of her friend that it was to Willa Mae that she confided her hopes about Mr. Johannson, shyly of course, almost afraid to put it into words. "Maybe—someday—"

When Eva Jean accepted the teaching job, Willa Mae suddenly decided to become a teacher too.

Until that very moment, Willa Mae had hated school. She was tired of it, she didn't want to spend another minute in it. But all of a sudden it was Eva Jean who would receive the salary of $50.00 per month, and Eva Jean who was talking about going on to get a teaching certificate at Chautauqua Institute. Suddenly, with no "prospects" to speak of herself, Willa Mae decided she too wanted to be a teacher. But of course, she wanted to be a teacher in a bigger town, and nicer school with smarter children than those that her friend would be teaching.

"Mama you want me to meet someone nice and how can I in this tiny town? I need to go somewhere else, and teaching is very respectable."

Her father had many friends. He spoke to a few of them, and they spoke to some others and soon it appeared that there was a teacher's job available north of the Platte. Willa Mae interviewed for it with the handsome young principal and was hired. It paid better than the little school in Elm Creek and Willa Mae was very pleased with herself.

While Eva Jean read, took her certificate at institute and planned out her year for her scholars, Willa Mae bought herself some new clothes, prepared a fine wardrobe to take with her, and relaxed before she was to start her taxing new job.

Chapter Four

The Teacher

October 27, 1912

I like my little scholars just fine. I like to think I might be helping them and contributing something of myself to our place here. Little Willie is still rigglin' around but he's learning, and Joseph is a great help carrying things and he's patient with the little ones. He is a smart boy. Should go on to more learning, but I spose he'll just stay on the farm. Anna is bossy still, but when I give her some real responsibility she will do it fine and the others are beginning to see she really is smart. And she is helping Sarah. Now if Sarah would only stop her whining. Good night little journal.

They called her Mizz Eva, right from the very first day, and it seemed natural that suddenly she was their teacher and not just another one of them. She knew them all so well.

Little Willie was 8, and a difficult student. He couldn't sit still no matter how hard he tried. He would wiggle and fidget and distract the others and the former teacher, Mr. White, constantly disciplined him and even used the paddle but it never helped. Eva Jean had dried his tears many times as a fellow student so he liked her. But how could she ever control him?

Sarah was 10, quiet and extremely shy. She had great difficulty reading, and was very poor at math. Mr. White had called on her to read often and made her sit on a high stool in front of the whole class when she couldn't read. She was terrified. Eva Jean was sure she would never be able to pass the simplest tests if things continued on in the same way. How could she help her to learn?

Joseph Huffman was 15. He was very big and strong and it had been a struggle to get his father to let him stay in school another year. Mr. Huffman wanted him on the farm. He didn't believe that Joseph needed any more schooling, and he certainly needed an extra pair of strong hands to work the acreage. At last he had agreed to let Joseph attend for one more year, only because Joseph told him he believed he could learn more about farming if he had just enough education to help him get into a mail order program. Then he could continue his schooling during the winter months. He was smart and eager and Eva Jean was relieved that he was continuing. She wanted to give him as much as he could handle and only hoped that she knew enough to get him the right books.

Anna was 12. She was large and awkward and self-conscious. She was one of the few who was an only child of older parents and she didn't have much in way of social skills. But she loved learning, so she was often bossy and overbearing with the others. Mr. White had tried to support her by praising her constantly. But he made it seem as if she was his pet and the others resented her for it.

The other nine students were just regular kiddies; some smarter and faster than others, all at different levels of learning; but Eva loved the challenge ahead of her.

But it was a challenge.

"I don't know Auntie. Willie is just maddening. He just won't sit still. I felt sorry for him when I was sitting next to him, but now that I'm the one in front of the class—why, he's just impossible. What am I going to do? Why won't he sit still?"

"Hmm. Glad it's not my job girl. You know, I remember Willie when he was just a baby. He couldn't lay still in the crib either. He was always rutchin' around. I remember one time when he was just 9 or 10 months old, he got loose in church and went under all the pews. Nobody could catch him. Maybe he just can't sit still-ever think of that?"

That gave Eva Jean an idea.

"Now then. We're going to read aloud. Willie, why don't you just stand in the back of the room behind the class, instead of trying to sit still? You can pace around if you want, but keep your attention up here. Does anyone mind if we let Willie stand?"

The students were relieved not to have him wiggling around next to them, so they approved. Willie needed the space, and gradually he sat down as she read but still had space to himself to move. It worked and Eva Jean tried every thing she could think of to keep his focus, but give him a chance to move around. It seemed to help him. She let him stand to work on his numbers instead of sitting. He was so relieved to know he wouldn't be hit, that little Willie adored her. He'd do anything for his Miz. Eva, even try harder than ever to stay in one place. He would wiggle from his shoulders to his toes standing in one place. But stay there he did.

Eva Jean didn't know what to do about Sarah so she didn't put any pressure on her at all for several weeks. Then she asked her to sit near her when she read. But she noticed that the others felt excluded, so she knew that wouldn't work so she tried something different. Instead of sitting in front as she read, which all her teachers had done before, she took to walking around, stopping by a different desk and asking that person to read aloud. Every once in a while she'd ask Sarah to read, just a word. At first Sarah couldn't do that either, but as she got comfortable and she knew that Eva wasn't going to ask her to read a hard word, she began to try.

Dear little Journal: I thought it was hard to help Aunt Stella all day long, but this teaching is harder than I could have dreamed. I think that most of my little class accept me all right. Willie is trying and Sarah is relaxing a bit. But Anna hates me.

Yes she does, she hates me. How can I get through to her? Maybe I'm trying too hard.

She knew that Anna could be a good teacher someday, but that she needed to gain respect. But Anna was jealous of Eva Jean. She was 12 yrs old, and she felt so big and so ungainly. Why should she listen to this tiny teacher who was really just one of them? But Eva would keep trying. Maybe she'd find the way. Sarah was much too afraid of big Anna to want to work with her— yet. But Eva Jean hoped that she could get them together gradually. She knew it would take time.

She came up with a great idea to study arithmetic. Her piece-work was second nature to her and she realized that making patterns of the triangles and rectangles and squares that made up much of quilting was a way to teach geometry. As usual there was no money for supplies, so she saved the sturdy brown paper that Aunt Stella's supplies came in, ironed it out and used it as the basis for her class to design carefully measured quilt squares, while she taught them math at the same time. The older ones helped the younger and the littlest ones colored in the paper with water-colors. Next year, she thought, she'd ask for crayons.

They worked at it a little each day, then they would sew the squares together with twine to make a kind of paper quilt to display for the parents. It worked out well. Joseph was working on geometry as he helped the younger ones.

Then one day Uncle Elroy said:

"Eva Jean what on earth are you doing over at that school ? All the men are talking about their boys making quilts. What's that all about?"

"We're not making quilts we're—Well, they look like quilts but,—Oh dear."

Dear Little Journal There's a problem with my quilt project. Now what am I going to do?

She was very tired in school the next day after laying awake most of the night trying, unsuccessfully, to come up with a solution to her great math project

Sure enough, at the end of the day she looked out the window to see Joseph's father standing on the porch.

"Oh, dear," she thought. "I'm not ready for this."

He had ridden the buckboard four miles to the school raising clouds of dust behind him as he drove, planning to talk some sense into this girl—or else.

He sent Joseph home and she invited him in.

"Can I help you Mr. Huffman?" she asked politely.

"I'll get right to the point. I've talked to the other fathers and we all feel the same way. We won't have our boys doing quilts. It's woman's work. Not right for our sons. Now I want this stopped right now. Didn't let Joseph stay here this year to learn this stuff."

Eva Jean was quiet. She pondered for a minute arguing with him. But instead she said.

"Well now, I understand you very well. Of course, you do know that we are learning math as we work with the shapes, but if you aren't happy with the boys doing that, we'll change it at once."

Mr. Huffman thought she would argue with him and was surprised.

The brown, unpainted paper shapes lay near her desk and she stared at them as an idea gathered in her head. The pause lengthened and just as he was about to challenge her again, she raised her eyes and said,

"In fact, Mr. Huffman, I would like to move on to something quite different for the boys. I'd like them to draw up the planting fields for us. Something like this plan here on the desk. They could do their measurements that way, and we can display the layout of the farms along with the girls work. What would you think of that?"

"Well now. I don't know—I suppose—Plan out fields of crops you say?"

Eva Jean's head was buzzing with ideas all at once, and suddenly she added, "Yes Sir, and I wonder if you might be able to help us. Later on, after the seasons over, when you have more time, I wonder if you could join us here at school and talk about the work of farming. You are our expert on planting and the weather and economics."

He looked puzzled. "Economics?" he said.

"Well, yes Sir. You can talk about what it is like to sell your produce; explain what makes a good year. Tell us how prices change. The students could really learn a lot from a man as experienced as you."

Suddenly, Mr. Huffman was beaming from ear to ear. Completely disarmed, he had in one short minute, become another one of Miss. Eva's strongest supporters.

He invited Eva Jean to ride with him, and left her at the doorstep of Aunt Stella's house.

She bounced in the door, and her aunt said.

"Well what on earth is Mr. Huffman doing with you?—and smiling yet. That old grouch has always got some complaint or other."

Eva Jean knew she'd done good. She knew she'd won him over and that she had also foiled someone who could have been a real enemy.

"I made a friend, Auntie. And most of all, I got a nice special program for my students, and I can keep our quilt project, and the boys will do the almost same thing, only we'll call it Planting the Fields. I'm learning, Auntie, I'm learning!"

Chapter Five

And The Dreamer

November 1, 1912

Dear Little Diary. Thomas has gone now, and I am lonely except for my kiddies and my dear Auntie and Uncle. I wish to hear from Willa Mae. Why hasn't she written? Well now, maybe I should of known better, but I've sent her many letters. It's cold now and the walk to school cold as ever it was. My boots chill my feet something awful. Glad I have warm petticoats though. Making a waist with dainty pin tucks on it for my hope chest. Without Willa Mae there's no one to show it to. My "hope" is that Willa is doing fine. Somehow it's hard to picture her as a teacher. Good Luck Willa Mae!

"Saw Mrs. Arnott today Eva Jean." Aunt Stella said, as Eva came in the door after school. "She says Willa Mae is real good. Says she has 15 students in the fifth grade and is liking it fine. Has a new beau too—older fella' I guess. Principal or something."

She wondered how it was going for her. Eva Jean was open and accepting of others and she was surprised but happy that Willa Mae wanted to teach and had found a job right away. But she was no fool. She knew that her friend hadn't really liked school very much although she was smart and learned quickly. She grew bored very quickly and she had little patience.

Willa Mae had found Little Willie's restlessness extremely annoying and secretly was pleased Mr. White gave him a licking. "Served him right." she thought. She had had no patience for Sarah's problems either. She called her the "little know-nothing." Eva Jean wondered how her friend was going to cope with 15 different students.

"Ah well," she thought. "She'll probably just bat her eyes at them and have them all eating out her hand in no time."

Then Willa Mae's letter arrived. November 19, 1912

Dearest, darling, Eva Jean,

My darling, best ever friend. I miss you SO much! I can't wait to see you and tell you all about Mr. Long. He is so handsome you wouldn't believe it. And he's much more interesting than any of the silly boys our own age. He is 25, very mature and experienced. He has been teaching a long time and they made him principal of our little school just last year.

We can't be seen together outside of school of course. So we meet in class after school and he helps me with my work. It's very romantic.

Hope you are happy in dreary old Elm Creek. Is Anna still bossing all the others? Hope you can manage her.

Hugs and kisses Miss Evie from your loving friend.

Willa Mae

Eva Jean smiled. Willa hadn't answered one question about her scholars and her teaching that Eva had asked her. But, oh my, her Mr. Long sounded very interesting.

She couldn't have known that Willa Mae's experience as a teacher wasn't worth writing about. While Eva had spent much of the summer preparing to teach, Willa Mae worked on her wardrobe. She faced her class with enthusiasm and sincerity, convinced she could stay ahead of them by planning as she went along. She was quite sure she could rule them with her adorable personality. Her dimples had never failed her yet. She knew exactly how to charm them. She would flirt with the boys and charm the girls with her impeccable clothes. The girls could admire her skill keeping the boys in line and she would become an unforgettable model for them.

In two days it had all turned upside down. The boys laughed at her dainty voice, mimicked the tilt of her head as she glanced through her long eyelashes at them, a technique that had always worked before. Suddenly she had lost her temper and her voice went up to a high-pitched squeal, her face became red and she squinted with such fury that her eyes disappeared. The boys loved it. They plotted at lunch how to make it happen again, and they succeeded within an hour. From that day on, Willa Mae lost her temper at least once a day. Her classroom discipline was a disaster.

As for the girls, they thought her clothes much too fine for school and therefore thought she had hoity-toity ideas. They saw that she had tried to flirt with the boys and they didn't like it one bit. There wasn't one girl in the class who liked her at all.

But she hadn't really cared. Willa Mae had taken one look at the nice looking young Principal, with his piercing eyes and his black mustache and had set her cap for him.

It was perfectly true that Mr. Long spent each afternoon with her in the room. As her supervisor he tried desperately to help her write out lesson plans and discuss disciplinary options.

It was very pleasant to spend an hour with this pretty little Miss. She could dazzle with her dimples and her vulnerable dependence on him for his advice. But Mr.Long, although charmed, was also aware that his reputation and his job were on the line. He was a very serious education professional. It was he who had recommended hiring her after a brief interview and he did not want to get in trouble with the parents of her students.

He'd let nothing spoil his success. He knew that he had to walk a very fine line with his employees or, he could be fired by the town fathers who'd hired him and paid his salary. He would have liked to see this pretty Miss after hours, since she was by far the most adorable, prettiest girl he'd ever seen. But it was impossible.

Dear Willa Mae,

I am so happy to have your letter. Your Mr. Long sounds like such a fine fellow. It must be hard to do courting in the classroom after school! He is a clever fellow too. Thomas and I don't have those problems as he is gone now to Lincoln to sell cars. But even so, I had to be so proper when we are able to go to church or to the dances together. Could not even hold hands, and I had to dance with everyone else so it would look proper. Of course once I started teaching we could not be alone at all. Now working hard helps me as I miss Thomas so much. I do love my teaching so, that I will miss it when once I am married. But that is a long way off. I wonder if someday ladies like us will be able to be teachers and marry too. What a thought! I hope you like your kiddies. I really love our little old school. You should see how well Willie is doing now. You wouldn't believe it.

I miss you too, dearest friend
Your friend, Eva Jean

Willa stood with the letter in her hand shaking her head. What was her friend thinking of—to be a teacher and to be married too? What decent woman would even think of such a thing? That Eva Jean! She surely had strange ideas. Willa Mae would never make such a mistake. A woman's place was in the home, and she allowed her fantasy of her friendship with Mr.

Long to take wing. She would stop work of course, as soon as he declared his intentions, and then when she was the wife of the up and coming young principal she would enjoy a very special place in the community.

Chapter Six

December 1912

The Journal

> *Goodness me, there is so much to do what with helping Aunt Stella and trying to make a really good school for my kiddies. I do really love them. Will I ever love another class as much as this one? All my kiddies I know so well. Little Willie is such a devil, but he makes me laugh and he tries so hard. When will I see my Thomas again? I miss him so. I talked to him once on the telephone but it was so fuzzy and you never know who will be listening in. We write almost every day. Keeps me going. My needlework keeps me busy too. I finished Thomas' vest and more hankies for sisters and Aunt. Will give the best one to Willa Mae. Best gift for Uncle Elroy was to help out with paying board. They weren't going to take it, but I'm proud to say, I insisted. It's only right. Soon Thomas and I will be together again. Oh, it will be so fine. Can't wait for Christmas. Hoorah! IT'S CHRISTMAS!*

Her hands flew from one stitch to another. She got the material for Thomas' vest from the general store; a nice, solid wool tweed, very special and rare for the mid-west. It came all the way from England. She worked the buttonholes very delicately, each stitch matching the last, each knot placed next to the one before so it looked even. She couldn't wait to give it to him. Aunt Stella worried about her eyes, since it got dark so much earlier, so Stella and Elroy finished each day cleaning the kerosene lamps so that the light was as bright and clear as possible.

But Eva Jean worked with a happy heart. She hadn't seen Thomas since October but she had high hopes that he would be with her for Christmas.

In the meantime she saw Royal often. He had been hired by the Western Union Telegraph to become a telegraph operator and amazingly they had sent him to nearby Kearney to work out of the office there. He could get to Elm Creek fairly easily and he came as often as he could.

"How can you learn to speak in a language that isn't a language?" Eva Jean asked when he came. Royal showed her how Morse code worked. The dots and the dashes made letters and she was amazed at how fast he could make his index finger fly to spell out words. He brought the practice telegraph key that he used in his off—hours, perfecting his technique. He was pretty fast as it was, but his goal to be the fastest telegrapher ever. And he had to work to be accurate. He had to spell things right, and his grammar had to be good too, so he knew how to help people make their messages sing across the lines.

The phone lines had just been put in that summer following the telegraph lines. Phone service was complicated. There were many families on one line, and you had to let it ring several times to distinguish which family was being called. Uncle Elroy grumbled that it was an unnecessary expense, but even he could see the value of being able to contact someone in case of an emergency. Besides, he was lucky that the farm was so close to town so the lines could be extended to them. Most farms were just too far away. So he grumbled, but he paid the bill and gradually Aunt Stella and Eva Jean were getting used to having a rare phone call. Royal called the most often. He had a job and could afford it. But to call as far away as Lincoln was very expensive, so Eva Jean and Thomas still used the mails most of the time. Thomas had written that he would be visiting about the 20th.

Eva Jean had come home from school the 17th, tired after her long day with her scholars and her long walk home. She didn't pick up the sewing as usual, but after the dinner was done, she sort of collapsed on the one soft chair in the front parlor for a few minutes. She would catch her breath before going upstairs to her room where she planned to do her class plans for tomorrow and perhaps just a few stitches before going to bed.

The ringing of the phone slashed through the quiet familiar noises of the old farmhouse. "Oh, my gosh, Eva said. Is it for us?" She listened carefully and then the patterned ringing was clear that it was their number. She was so excited when she picked up the phone and heard his voice.

It was Thomas.

"Eva Jean, Eva Jean is that you? It's Thomas. Are you there?"

"Yes, Yes," she shouted to make herself heard over the cracking, humming phone line. "It's Me, It's Eva. Are you all right? Are you coming home?"

"Oh, Eva Jean, I'm so sorry. I can't make it."

"What? What? I can't hear you."

He almost bellowed the words this time. "I can't make it. I must stay and keep the office open Eva Jean. The other fella' here has a wife due to give birth. He can't be expected to stay. I'm sorry, but I'll try to get to you as soon as possible. Are you all right?"

"Yes, yes" she said. But her heart was in her shoes. The days had been so dark, so gloomy and the school so cold. She was so young and she longed to have just a bit of fun and laughter. Each day she came home and worked more, before falling exhausted into bed. How long before they could be together?

He heard the disappointment in her voice.

"Oh, I'm sorry, I'm so sorry." The line crackled, and faded as the wind outside whipped the lines.

"I'll write soon, I promise. Smile for me Eva Jean. Let me pretend I can see you."

She laughed in spite of herself and grinned. "I'm smiling" she said.

"I can hear it in your voice. Be good now." His voice faded. Did he say, I love you?

"What, What?" she almost shouted but he was gone.

Aunt Stella stood in the doorway.

"Oh dear, I'm sorry Eva Jean. He can't come. Is that it?"

She was in her arms in a minute. "I'm so disappointed."

She cried a little, but just a little. Wasn't seemly to cry over such a little thing. Not like the crops failed, or somebody died now was it? But still.

Christmas was quiet then. They exchanged one small gift each, had a nice dinner prepared by Stella and Eva Jean. Later she and Royal went by wagon to visit their sisters and spend some time with their families. They didn't get to see them often. They enjoyed their few hours together, sang songs at Leona's piano, and ate the fruit cake that Stella had made as a special treat.

Eva Jean was terribly lonely. She longed for some fun, some gaiety. She worked so hard all the time. She was either planning for her students, correcting their work, reading to keep herself up to date or doing her needlework which was truly relaxing for her. And if she wasn't busy enough with all of that, she was helping Aunt Stella with the meals, the laundry, the cleaning, or feeding the chickens or milking the cow. There were a hundred chores or more that were part and parcel of even the smallest working farm and Eva Jean loved her aunt and uncle so that she tried to do whatever she could.

They didn't take advantage of her. She brought them so much just by being herself, always with a smile, a quick remark, and her bright and sunny disposition. Still, there was so much to do, when she offered they didn't often stop her.

Willa Mae was home for two days. Eva Jean was thrilled to see her, but she talked so much about Mr. Long that even Eva Jean was annoyed with her.

"Mr. Long and I are going to be engaged before long. You'll see. Mr. Long and I have such wonderful discussions after school. Of course, we can't really see one another outside of school but we manage just fine, and when I'm married, I won't have to work and then it will be so wonderful. He's going to inherit some money soon and can buy his own house. Isn't that something? I'll have my own home. Oh, Eva Jean I hope you won't have to wait forever for Mr. Johannson."

Willa Mae was in her own world as usual. Nothing could spoil it. Nothing stood in her way. But she did just love her gift of the fanciest hanky Eva Jean had ever made. Somehow it seemed just right for Willa Mae and she kissed her for it, and was truly pleased.

Then suddenly the holiday was over, Willa Mae was gone, the weather was incredibly bleak and Eva Jean felt more alone than ever.

But all at once, as she sat once more with her piecework in her hands, she had an idea. It came to her in a flash and she sat up straight, the needle poised in her hand her eyes narrowed and fixed on a vision somewhere inside her head. It was a crazy idea, a daring idea. It was a way to see Thomas, a way to give him the gift she had worked so long to create for him, and if she did it just right it was also a way to protect her reputation.

There was no way she could travel to Lincoln alone. Even if Stella could go with her, the idea of her traveling to meet a man was not accepted.

Her idea was daring. She giggled to herself. She ran to the mirror and pulled her hair behind her and twisted it to the top of her head. She turned her head and smiled to herself in the mirror. Then she frowned and tried to look somehow different. Then she tossed her hair loose again, jumped up and down like a child and clapped her hands. "It'll work!" she said aloud. "It'll work. Now if I can only get Royal to help."

Chapter Seven

The Adventure

The Journal: December 1912

Little Journal I am going to tell you a secret that no one else must know. I am going to do something daring and wonderful. But I need my brother to help. How I hope that it will work. I miss my dear Thomas so much, and I need to see him. Life is so hard with the cold and so much work to do. It is a daring plan, but I am willing to risk it. May God bless my adventure, and keep me safe.

He thought it was absolutely crazy. It was the craziest idea he'd ever heard. The very idea! His sister dressed up like some guy. What on earth ever made her even think of such a thing?

"No. Absolutely not!" He'd told her. "Why, you'd look silly. No one would ever think you could be a boy. What would you wear? How could you get clothes? This is the worst idea you've ever had. Why, Eva Jean! What would people say? You'd lose your job. We'd all be shamed. I absolutely, positively will not help you in any way. No sirree, Bob."

But Eva Jean was not to be put off. She was desperate to see Thomas again. She knew exactly how she would get the clothes.

They would come from the poor basket at church. It was time for the usual collection to be gathered for the spring rummage sale, and she was in charge of it. She could borrow the old clothes for her adventure and return them before anyone even knew they had been used. She already had found a shirt and had it washed and cleaned. She would wear her own underclothes and stuff them into the knickers. There was an awful pair of boy's shoes that she could just squeeze her feet into and plenty of boy's stockings to chose from, although she'd have to scrub them really good, and there was just one cap that fit her. The cap of course was critical. It had to be big enough to push her hair into. She couldn't risk cutting her hair for this adventure no matter what.

By the time Royal was to come for Sunday dinner, the outfit was all ready. Just as dinner was prepared, she sneaked around the corner of the house, dressed quickly in the barn and met Royal as was coming up the road alongside the house. Her back was to him as he approached, and she slouched and walked as though she had been walking a long distance.

"Hi there!" Royal said as he came alongside. "Haven't seen you around here. Where you headed?"

"Town, I hope," was the answer.

"Oh, well you're way off. Got to go back a ways. Just keep on the road and you'll find your way right into town at the next turn.

"Thanks. Thanks a lot," the stranger answered and turned and started off the other way. He turned back once and waved as Royal stood looking at him.

He was in the house greeting his Aunt and Uncle, when Eva Jean came in the back door. She was full of delight at seeing him as usual, full of her laughter and charm—the very thing that endeared her to most people who knew her.

"Eva Jean did you see that young guy who was passing by?— about 16 he was. He was going the wrong way—looking for the town. I sent him back. Did you see him go by?"

"Nope, Didn't see him."

As Stella and Eva Jean went about getting the dinner, Uncle Elroy and Royal got into a long discussion about strangers. People were traveling all over the country now, by train mostly, and it changed their sense of security. Used to be you knew everyone you saw. Not any more.

They all sat down and dishes were passed back and forth until Royal passed the dish of potatoes to Eva Jean and she said. "Thanks, thanks a lot" and looked him right in the eye.

Royal's face turned nearly purple as he realized that the stranger was his sister and he had fallen for it. But he didn't dare say a thing in front of his aunt and uncle.

Later on he was as furious with her as it was possible for him to be. Which was hard. Royal adored her, plain and simple.

"But I would of knowed it was you if we'd talked more. And I really didn't look much in his,—I mean, your face."

"So, nobody else who sees me will have any notion who I am. You said yourself, I looked just like a 16 year old boy. We'll take the wagon to Leona's. We'll get them to take us to the train while we go for a day to Lincoln. We'll be back before the day is out and then we can drive the team home."

"Eva Jean it's out of the question. I don't have the money for two train tickets to Lincoln and back."

"But I do. I sold one of my small quilts to Mrs. Johns for her new grand baby. She was thrilled and I got the money. Come on, Royal do it for me. If I don't get out of here and see Thomas again, I'm going to go crazy. Just because I'm a teacher doesn't mean I can't have some fun does it?"

"Eva Jean, I just can't do this."

"Then I'll go alone."

Royal was floored. "Oh, Eva Jeannette. No."

"Yes, I will, I swear, I'll go alone."

She was lying of course. If he wouldn't take her she couldn't possibly do it alone, but she was so into her pretense that at that moment, she seemed so determined, so set on her way that Royal was simply overwhelmed.

Every step of the way was complicated. They chose the weekend and Royal wired Thomas that he would be in town and wanted to see him, and Thomas wired back that he would meet him after hours at the car garage. They told their Aunt and Uncle that they were going to visit their sister and told their sister that Royal was going to accompany her to Lincoln just for a day. They argued about how she would change her clothes—and where she would change her clothes. She didn't know the answer to that one, but she'd figure it out as she went.

In the end she changed her clothes on the train in the bathroom room just off the corridor with Royal sweating just outside the door. He'd almost fainted when she went in the room as a woman, and nearly fainted again when she came out 15 minutes later as a boy. He'd been sure at least two men who came down the corridor had wanted to use the bathroom but they had just passed on by.

He relaxed a bit as they met people who didn't give her another glance. With her hair up and strong clean face, she did look like a boy. Royal wondered how she managed to get her chest so flat, but he certainly wasn't going to ask. Actually she had bound herself up with a strip from an old sheet.

It was dusk when they reached the car lot full of wonderful new machines. Royal approached Thomas nervously. He hadn't planned on what he was going to say to him, or how he would explain this crazy scheme. He had just been as sure as Eva Jean was that Thomas was going to be thrilled to see her again. That was all that mattered. She figured she'd have an hour or two with him, then Royal would meet them somewhere and they'd reverse their journey.

Thomas was really glad to see Royal. His face just beamed. He grasped his hand and covered their handshake with the other. It was like having a little piece of her here to see this brother of hers.

"This is wonderful. How great it is to see you. Can you dine with me? I reserved a table at the boarding house. How's Eva Jean? How're you? I'm so sorry I couldn't get back for Christmas, but I'm going to surprise Eva Jean next weekend. What do you think Roy? Does she miss me?"

"Well—ah—that's what I came about. Next weekend did you say? Oh God. Well—she thought—that is"—

Thomas had spotted the boy lingering behind Royal.

"Who's this?" He reached out his hand and she instinctively reached to him.

She looked up into his face, nervous, but sure he would be pleased. She was so happy to see him again, to see that he was just as nice looking as she had remembered, his grey eyes so bright, his nose so straight and fine, and his hair all full and fair curling across his forehead, that she smiled and said just simply.

"It's me."

He actually jumped back as he dropped her hand.

"No! Oh, my God! Oh, NO!"

"I'll just leave you for now. Eva, I'll be around the corner. You make your plans." Royal said and he disappeared.

His tone frightened her.

"You're not mad? But he just stared at her.

"Oh, please don't be mad Thomas. I was so lonely, and I talked Royal into this. Please just say you're not mad at me. I just missed you so. I thought we'd just have an hour or so. It was better than nothing—I"—

Eva Jean stopped. She looked at his face, and waited for him to say something. He was stunned. There she stood in front of him, the girl of all of his dreams. She looked outlandish in those knickers and ugly shoes. Why you could see her ankle shape under the bulky stocking. He looked at her sweet face, the curve of her neck under the cap—her ear. He'd never really seen her ear before.

Eva Jean turned pale. Around the corner, Royal stood waiting to hear his voice. He was too far away to hear what he would say, but something told him this wasn't going well. If he just heard his voice he'd know how he was taking it.

And then he heard it. The tone was low and urgent, not gentle. It was not a lover's voice. Royal groaned inside and put his face in his hands.

"My God in heaven, Eva Jean what on earth are you thinking? Yes I wanted to see you, but not like this. You look—You look—

Why—I don't know what to say. What if someone sees you? Why, I'll be ruined. You'll be ruined. How could Royal?—What on earth were you two thinking of.

"Oh, Thomas don't. We have so little time and I risked so much to come to you. Please don't." The words were whispered. But it was as if he didn't even hear her.

Now he was speechless. He just stared at her. She reached up and slowly took off the cap and shook out her hair.

A little groan escaped his lips. There was an inexplicable look on his face.

"You see. It's still just me Thomas, just Eva Jean. Same as always."

But it wasn't just Eva same as always. Before him stood this woman; this incredibly beautiful, adorable woman who had gone through god knows what to get to him. But—

"No!" He said. No! Not like this. Go home, Eva Jean. Just go home!"

She stood there, cap in hand, as Thomas turned and walked away from her. She didn't see the tears in his eyes. She didn't hear the choked sound in his throat as he fought them back. He walked away quickly, rubbing his head with his hands as if he had a headache. She just stared after him without moving until he was gone and until finally Royal was next to her his arm around her shoulder leading her away.

Thomas went inside, put on a coat and scarf, remembered to turn out the lights, walked outside again and just kept going. He didn't think. Didn't know where he was going. His chest hurt and he couldn't think straight. The light dimmed and he saw the lamp lighter start his rounds. Thomas barely noticed. He turned a corner in a section of town he hadn't been in before. It was near the place of business where he worked, but it wasn't a nice place. There were rumors of the kinds of people who lived there and the kind of work they did.

Music drifted from a house down a ways. It was the new music from down south, jazzy and brash, but with rhythm, and it pounded almost like his heart was pounding. He was near the door of the house now. It had been a simple home once as town was growing. Probably was a small farm behind it, but now it was just another worn out, unpainted old place. Laughter poured out the door and light glowed from all the windows up and down.

He knew what it was. All the men he worked with were talking about it. Just a few weeks earlier some men had arrived from down South with sheet music and three women with them. They'd moved into this old place and rumors were flying. The women were trashy and loud and dressed bold. The men all knew who they were and why they were there but so far no one Thomas knew had visited the place.

All at once the door opened and a woman came out. Thomas stopped in his tracks. She was laughing and she saw him and called out.

"Hi there honey, come on in. Don't be shy."

It all happened pretty fast. He just got a glimpse of bare shoulders and then she pulled her shawl around her. Then he saw her feet. She was bare footed. Bare footed on the porch. Her ankle was showing—a bare ankle. Thomas had never seen a bare foot or ankle on a woman before. Girls, yes, when they were kids, but a woman—! A man could dream about a woman's legs— they were a mystery. And there she was—this woman inviting him in. She saw him look at her legs and laughed and hitched up her skirt.

"Come on in, honey, it's cold out here." She reached out her hand.

"I'll warm ya' up, all right."

He didn't see her face really. He couldn't tell you if she was young or old, or if her hips were slim or wide, but he saw that ankle and that foot and suddenly something else too.

He saw Eva Jean before him—her ankles covered in those boy's stockings, he saw her ear, her neck.

The woman was losing patience.

"Hurry up now. It's too cold out here" and she gave a little dance.

"You won't be sorry."

But Thomas was off and running the other way.

"Damn!" the woman muttered. "Whats' a matter sonny? Sceered?

Chapter Eight

Regrets

"What have I done? I sent her away. I insulted her. I let her think I only cared about what people would say." He groaned aloud as he ran. "She came all this way. I must be out of my mind." He was running back to the lot where the cars sat and found the one he'd driven that day trying to make a sale. He moved like a mad man, cranking it up and jumping back and forth to get it to catch and start and then he was off.

The car made it to the block before the station where it wheezed and died. Out of gas. He groaned and cursed, but jumped out and ran the rest of the way to the station. She was sitting alone in the very back of the waiting room, in the pew-like bench slumped in a corner. Somehow, wearing pants made her feel so different that she didn't even sit like a girl, straight with both her feet on the floor. She leaned over her knees, just like a boy with her head in her hands.

When she looked up sensing his presence more than seeing him there, she felt suddenly stupid and ashamed and she turned away from him at once, embarrassed that he should see her again in the garb she now considered ridiculous. She pulled the cap low on her head, crossed her arms over her chest, and pulled her knees together. But he was next to her in an instant.

"Oh. Eva Jean, please forgive me. Please. I was such a fool. It's just—I was so shocked—I didn't know what to do."

"No," she answered. "No, you were right. What will people think?"

"I don't care what people think. I was longing to see you, but I never dreamed you'd be so eager to see me too. I—I—I'm sorry", he said sitting next to her, looking once more at the back of her neck, that sweet curve of her neck where her hair just curled in little wisps.

"We came all this way," she said, quietly, feeling calmer now that he was there, but hurt too. How could he? She just looked at him.

"I know Eva Jean, I'm so sorry, please forgive me. I spoiled it. We had so little time."

Royal came around the corner just then and saw them through the window. His first instinct was to punch Thomas right in the nose. But he realized all at once that Eva Jean was looking at him with that bright-eyed look that meant something special was going on. Thomas was holding her hand by then, so Royal stayed outside in the cold and paced up and down watching to see if anyone was coming. Every once in a while he'd peek through the window at them.

What a sight they made! A young man, handsome, just 20 now, looking with gentle eyes at a younger boy—holding his hand even. Royal was a nervous wreck. What if someone came? Jeez, what would they think? The next time he looked, the cap was off, and there sat the younger boy with a tumble of fabulous hair over his shoulders looking like—what? Like a girl that's what. A girl dressed like a boy. She could get arrested!

Someone was coming and Royal couldn't stand it another minute. He grabbed the bag he held with all her clothes, dashed in and plunked her hat back on her head.

"Change! NOW!" Royal demanded. And Eva Jean grabbed the bag and ran to the bathroom to become a girl once more.

When she came back, slightly disheveled from the rush, the two men sat side-by-side sharing a cig.

"We've got about five minutes. I'll wait for you on the track Eva Jean. Don't be late, we've got enough problems."

"Thanks Royal," Thomas said. "Thanks for everything." And they shook hands.

"You didn't think much of me as a boy. Is this any better?" She asked.

"I think you're adorable no matter what Eva Jean." Her face just glowed. "Adorable, he thinks, I'm adorable," she thought to herself.

The word was incredibly special coming from him. A word he'd probably never even said before, and one no one had ever used to her.

"I'll make it up to you somehow," he promised. "I'll get to you next weekend somehow. You can be sure I will."

He stood for a long time on the platform and watched the train pull away until the red light on the caboose faded away.

The next day, Thomas lost his job.

January 1913

Well, little journal, here I am again in a whole new year. It worked! My scheme to see my beau worked even though it was a near thing! I got to see him and it was fine. And no body was the wiser. Except maybe me. I won't try that again. Besides Royal will kill me if I do. He said I was "adorable" Thomas did. Can you imagine? Me? Adorable! Oh I can't wait to see Thomas again. Soon!!!

Chapter Nine

Together Again

Elroy heard it first—the sound of the car coming from far down the road that passed just by their house. He lifted his head from the field where he was walking, preparing for the first planting. He frowned.

"What the?" but he knew. He'd heard the noise of the things in the market towns now, although no one near Elm Creek had one yet. The chug, chug of it, the purr of the engine was new, challenging the one familiar engine they had become accustomed to. They were so familiar with the trains that they had become the town clock. People within hearing distance knew exactly when they were coming and set their watches by it. There's the 1:15, they said—lunch over, time to get back to work. Even Eva Jean paced her school day by the distant sound of the train, excusing her students for lunchtime, or an afternoon recess by its familiar hoo—eeey. Often it beat the chickens at waking the citizens of each little town. At 5:58 a.m. every single person, young and old woke up as the train went through blowing its whistle. People could have been divided into those who got up at once and started the day, and those who loved to lie in the warmth of their own beds listening to the sound; the churning, the sharp curve of the whistle as it sped away and faded slowly into the distance; fading into silence once more.

But this car thing was another sound altogether. But then Elroy realized that it would be Eva's young man coming to call, and he chuckled.

Thomas was already at the house by the time Eva Jean came home from school. She had arranged for Mr. Morton to bring her home in the buckboard so she didn't have to walk. He was glad to do it for her. Little Sarah was his daughter and he could see how she was blossoming under Eva Jean's patient teaching.

He was amazed at the car. Eva Jean and Thomas stood looking at one another, each of them, grinning, shy, excited to see one another, and pretending a patience neither of them had as Mr. Morton "ohhhed" and "aahhed" over the car. Thomas showed him how it worked and let him sit in it for a few minutes. Finally he left. Thomas reached out his hand just as soon as the buckboard passed out of distance. She took it and they murmured their greetings. Stella watched from inside the house, smiling to herself.

"Oh my," she said. "My oh, my. Our girl has herself a real fella' all right."

"Your Aunt was so kind to me. We've had tea, and her cake. She's some baker I guess." Thomas said.

"Yes, yes indeed. Did you like her cake? I'll have her teach me, then I can make it just for you."

"I'd like that."

Still they faced one another, and held hands and didn't move.

"Can we take a walk do you think?"

"Yes, yes, I'll get my shawl. Don't go away."

Breathless, she was inside in a minute and Aunt Stella stood at the doorway already holding the shawl.

"Go on now—Take a walk. Mind yourself though". It was a loving admonition.

Eva Jean blushed to the roots of her hair and Aunt Stella laughed her hearty, warming laugh.

"Oh my", she said. "Don't be out too long, It's cold now."

The truth was, it was very cold, but once in the house they wouldn't have a minute alone together so they walked to the barn, turned the corner and—somehow it just happened. Thomas was just ahead of her. He turned just as she stepped around the corner and she bumped right into him. He put his arms around her then, started to ask if he could kiss her, but her face was so close, her eyes so shining, and the kiss just came before either of them had time to think.

Eva Jean was just lost in that kiss. It was warm and soft, and long, and she was aware of his arms around her, and then his hands holding her head, warming her ears, and his breath warm as he kissed her in tiny, impatient little kisses, her cheeks, her lips, her eyes. Her knees buckled. And he reached around her again to hold her up, leaned her gently against the barn and kissed her again.

"Eva Jean, I love you. I love you."

Her voice was just a whisper. "Yes, yes, love me," she said. Then she laughed. "Oh, please. Love me."

And how he would have loved to love her, right then and there. Love her with his kisses and his arms and—

With a strength Thomas only had for her, for his girl, his Eva Jean, he held her away from him, trying to let his heart stop pounding.

"We've got to get in before you catch your death."

"I'm fine." She looked up at him, at the fine young man who had said that he loved her and with her eyes closed and her face turned up at him, she said in a little voice just like her youngest student—

"Do—'gin"

And he did. He kissed her for the chance he had, for the long days they had never had together, for the yearning that he hadn't even known he'd felt until he saw her last weekend in that boy's suit.

"That's to keep you warm for awhile," he said.

She couldn't answer him. She really couldn't speak. But she took his hand as before and followed him back around the barn, across the yard to the house.

Stella took one look at her face and knew this was a girl who had been kissed. But she fussed at them both, took his coat, her shawl, settled them in around the big old stove, just as Elroy came in stomping and huffing, and blustering.

"Well, then, I see we've got one of those damned things right here." How're you doin' my boy? Like driving these things?

"Yes, Sir. It's not mine. I borrowed it for the weekend. Friend of mine. I sold it to him though."

"Is that right? That car business going all right then, I suppose."

"Yes Sir, yes Sir just fine". Somehow he couldn't tell them all yet. Tell them that he'd lost his job because he had taken a car to the station to see Eva Jean and it had run out of gas and he'd had to leave it there until the next morning.

His boss was dumbfounded that he'd taken it, and that he wouldn't explain why. Mr. Dodd had liked this boy. Yes, indeed liked him just fine. He was a good salesman. Had an honest face. People liked him and he'd been doin' just fine selling cars. But he couldn't possibly keep him on now. Impossible! The boy had taken a car without permission. Unheard of, it was. Intolerable. He was just lucky he didn't turn him in to the Sheriff.

Somehow Thomas would find a way to tell Eva Jean before the weekend ended, but now he just said.

"Well Sir, selling cars has been fine, but you know I been thinking that I could make a go of farming if I could get some land, and I heard that there's land west 'a here free to homestead. Thought I'd look into it and see if I could make a claim."

"That so? Elroy lit up his pipe. "Where you thinkin' of?"

"Colorado" Thomas said.

"Eva Jean almost stopped breathing and Aunt Stella almost fell off her chair. It was her worst nightmare. Eva Jean so far away—too far for them to be able to help her, and she knew she would need so much help. Quietly, Stella rose from the table and went into the kitchen.

"It's so far." Eva said.

"Not so far, only a day by train. And there's a train that connects to a place called Stoneham. Prairie Dog Special they call it."

The very idea of traveling that far by train was exciting and scary. Of course, no one she knew had traveled that far by train. Most people still drove by horse and wagon everywhere they went and a trip to Colorado was three days at least, depending on the weather. It seemed very far to her—Very far indeed. It had been bad enough having him in Lincoln. That was half a day away, and look what she had had to go through to get to see him.

But Thomas was excited.

"I thought that I could get settled there. I've heard that there could be a relinquishment of a homestead. If I'm there I'll have the first chance. Seems a lady tried to work it, but she couldn't and they say it's going to be up for grabs soon. A hundred and sixty acres. I'll stay there and get me whatever work I can till I got a stake and got some place to live. Eva Jean, what do you think? Do you want to be a farmer's wife? Would you want to go with me? You'll see, cars are going to make a big difference in travel and it'll be a faster trip before long. What'd, ya say?"

Eva Jean was still stunned by the idea. But she lifted her head, looked Thomas in the eyes and said,

"If it's what you want, yes I do. I love living on a farm. I'll make Aunt Stella's cakes for you and quilt till my fingers fall off! It's all I ever wanted Tom. How long do you think it'll take?"

She smiled up at him and tried not to let him see that she was nervous about it all. It was such a sudden change. Truth was she hadn't really thought about what it would be like to live away from the only family she had, Aunt Stella and Uncle Elroy, and Royal. But as she sat there watching him talk about what he might farm, about how he could get a good piece of land or so he'd heard, and she saw how excited he was, she relaxed. For him, for her Thomas, she could wait. She could be anything he wanted. It would be all right.

The weekend sped by. He used the car to drive to Royal's to stay with him on Sat., came back Sunday for church, and dinner and then he was gone. There had been a chance for one more kissing episode and by the time it ended, Eva Jean was breathless, longing for more and happier than she'd ever been in her life.

Thomas left wearing the vest she'd made for him, promising he'd write as soon as he was settled. He'd call her too.

"I don't like the telephone, Thomas", she'd said. "It doesn't sound like you, it's so far away and there's so much noise on the line and who knows who's listening in. The whole town will know our business. I like a letter better."

"I know. But it's better than nothing, and it may take me awhile to get settled. I've got some money I saved so I ought to be OK for a while. And I'll pick up work where I can. Don't forget me Eva Jean."

"As if I could."

It was the last kiss and then Uncle Elroy was there, and Aunt Stella with a piece of cake for the road, and he was gone, the car chugging along, leaving a trail of smoke behind. He didn't turn around but he waved back at her over his head and she waved too even though he couldn't see it.

Eva Jean's eyes burned with tears, and her throat felt like she'd swallowed a huge ball. But she had a big, brave smile on her face when she turned back to her Aunt. Stella didn't say a word, but put her arm around her and led her into the house.

In their own room, Stella and Elroy sat together on the edge of their own bed. He held her quietly, and rocked her gently as the quiet tears streaked down her lined and careworn face.

"Now, there my girl, don't you cry. Our Eva Jean will be all right. You'll see. She loves this fella and he's going to work hard for her. She's a strong girl. Tiny thing, but strong. Our girl will be fine. Ssshh," Elroy whispered. "Ssshh."

The journal said:

January 30, 1913

Thomas said good-bye and I will miss him so. But oh, what fine things we will have to look forward to someday, when we never have to say goodbye again. I'm doing the sixth square now. Our quilt will be done long before we set a date.

Chapter Ten

Willa's Dream

Journal Entry: Date: March 12, 1913

I miss Thomas terribly. Letters are so slow now with the weather and all, and they are all I have of him. Mine may not get to him for weeks. Working hard at school, and with my precious sewing—all things for our future together. Tired to the death. No news from Willa Mae and I write and write. Wonder how she is doing now.

The door closed behind him and Vernon Long continued to watch his teachers and the last of the students from the window in the very corner of the small brick building that was his school. He hoped he'd see her leaving with the others. Where was she?

Many days—too many days, Willa Mae stayed behind to talk to him.

"I wonder," she'd say. "Can you help me?"

And each time her problem related to a student who was unruly or disrespectful or who just wouldn't learn. And when he spoke with the student's former teachers, they usually were surprised that the child was having such difficulties.

"John is bit of a talker, but he was never rude." They said, or "Susan! Not doing her work! Why she was always so eager!"

He knew the teachers were beginning to talk about Willa Mae's problems. He knew they were even aware of how much she sought him out. It was unusual. Teachers usually supported one another; they didn't run to the Principal every time there was a problem. But he liked his pretty little Miss Arnott. She made him feel handsome and wise. She was so earnest in her desire to improve as a teacher, and she tried to take his suggestions.

Poor Vernon. His brow furrowed as he stroked his fine mustache and shook his head. So disturbing were his thoughts of her that he never heard her enter, and his sigh masked the sound of her skirts as she closed the door behind her.

He actually jumped when her heard her voice.

"Oh, dear Sir, your job is so very difficult. I shouldn't be bothering you with my problems." She started to go, which meant that of course, he had to stop her.

"No, no—That's quite all right,—Always time for you Miss Arnott. Please do sit down."

But his head was saying, "Damnation!"

He didn't want to deal with her. But then—

There she was before him, adorable as always, her dark hair framing her perfect face, the lips so pink you might think—but no, no. There wouldn't be any rouge on her lips. It was all just Willa.

She smiled in that way that made the little dimples at the corner of her lips, wink at him and her head tilted ever so slightly.

All thoughts of his profound disturbance just being with this girl, disappeared when she sat on the edge of the chair. He noted her round shape curving down to the tiny waist; her plump little wrist draped so casually over the arm of the chair, her shoe just peeping out from the edge of her skirt.

He allowed himself to relax in her presence. Why not? Why not just enjoy her? He was, after all, the professional, her superior in every way. He was the man in control of his school, his teachers, and her job. He sighed again, adjusted his chair, leaned back and resting his arms on the chair, his fingertips touching, he smiled at her.

She saw his eyes relax, the little crinkles appear at the corners as she recognized the smile she was beginning to know so well. He always seemed ill at ease at first, and then she'd see him relax. She believed that she was good for him; that she helped him cope with a difficult job full of worry and stress. Willa arranged her skirts. "Take your time," she told herself. "Make it last."

He watched her as she looked into her lap, the little crease form above her nose as she frowned ever so slightly. But she didn't speak.

"Well now," he said. "And how did things go today?"

She explained carefully how she had taken his suggestion to speak slower, to keep facing her class and to occasionally walk among the students instead of remaining in the front. It had been a much better day, and she described her plan for them and how cleverly she had told them a story to illustrate how much they could gain if they paid attention.

He watched her talk, nodded and smiled his encouragement. He barely heard what she said, only how she looked and sounded. He almost missed her question.

"Beg pardon?" he asked. She repeated it.

"Do you think I ought to accept the invitation to dine at home with Erdine's family? They don't have much I don't think, and I don't know if I should really have them cook for me, but they asked me to come to talk about her work."

"Yes, why yes, I think that's a good idea. It always helps to find out just how our students live at home, and the fact that they asked you is very encouraging. You wouldn't want to disappoint them." He rose from his seat knowing that he really must end this interview.

She took the hint. "Oh dear, I mustn't keep you. Thank you so much for your help. I don't know what I would do without it. It keeps me going." He had it in mind to tell her to wear something very simple. Willa had a way of overdressing that might seem condescending to such simple people

They were at the door before he realized how close they were, standing suddenly face to face. She looked up at him—there was that smile, and the head tilted and—he quite forgot what he had meant to say.

It all happened so suddenly he didn't realize what he was doing till his lips were leaving hers and the smell of her dazzled his senses.

He'd kissed her. Suddenly—just like that, he had kissed the girl ! And she had responded and he didn't pull away just exactly—fast.

"Why, Mr. Long."

"I—I—forgive me my dear, I just—I just"—He really couldn't speak. Had he just called her "my dear?" My God, he must be mad.

He was behind the defenses of his desk in a second, but she followed him.

"Oh, I understand. It's all right. I feel it too. I do. Oh Vernon, at last to know how you feel."

At the sound of her using his first name his heart bounded. This was so inappropriate, so completely wrong that he just blurted.

"Oh No. Oh no—you mustn't—please don't."

"It's really quite all right. It's just our secret. I'd never tell a soul. It wouldn't be right. Please, you can rely on me. I'll be a little mouse you'll see. But I'm so happy. And I won't come to you. You can see me whenever you wish in my own room."

She was babbling now, but so happy that she was just thrilled to the core of her tiny—waisted dress. It was what she had dreamed. It was going to be all right now. She had what she'd wanted the most.

She whirled to the door almost jumping for joy, and then she blew him a kiss in the sweetest way, and she was gone.

Vernon's heart was almost beating out of his chest. He fell into his chair. His head sank to the desk.

"My God, what have I done," he moaned. "What have I done?"

Chapter Eleven

The Dream Unraveled

March 19, 1913

My dear Eva Jean,

Mr. Long has made his intentions very clear to me. I must keep it all secret for now. No one must know, but you, dear Eva, you I have to tell for I am bursting with pride. To think that he, the Principal of our school should pick me! He's such a fine gentleman, so careful in his dress, so polite and well spoken.

Dare I tell you? Oh, I must. His kiss was so swift and gentle I was breathless. I suspect it won't be long now, as the year comes to an end that we can admit the truth to one and all and make our plans. I am so happy, but I can't even tell my parents.

Oh, do keep my secret. I know I can trust you.

Your friend forever,
Willa Mae

But something was happening that Willa, who was accustomed to getting her way; who never failed once she made up her mind, couldn't understand. Mr. Long wasn't coming to her room as she believed he would. He wasn't seeking her out at all. In fact he seemed to be avoiding her. It was a week—a whole five days. Willa had had the supper with the parents of her student. It had gone well although, as Mr. Long had guessed, she had dressed all wrong, wearing her nicest party dress to a dreary little house without even a separate room for the table. She had sat in the kitchen, looking like a little princess, supremely out of place. Little Erdine was overwhelmed and couldn't even speak. But even so, Willa Mae's sweet smile, her serious encouragement of her student, her very polite small talk had impressed the parents greatly. In truth they were awed by her; the father tongue-tied in her presence. But the mother was proud of her best cloth on the table, sure that she would notice and to her credit, Willa Mae did, commenting on how very pretty the table looked, set with such a nice cloth. That put the mother at ease and the two women had gotten along quite well.

Dinner was a chicken stew, made rich with cream from the family's one cow, and cooked long enough to soften the scrawny old hen they had slaughtered for the occasion. The biscuits were light and delicious, and although their store of potatoes was long gone, there were carrots browned and buttery. An apple pie finished the meal. Willa Mae was most impressed.

She couldn't wait to tell Vernon. But where was he?

He was beside himself with anxiety. Each day he left the school early. He told his secretary to let him know if Willa came by the office, although she did not do that for the first time since she'd been teaching. She remained in her classroom each day after classes waiting for him, and he never came.

By the end of the week Willa was almost ill with anxiety.

"Why'd I have to go and tell Eva Jean of all people?" she fumed silently. "She's all set with her beau, and I go bragging about mine. Why hasn't he come to see me?"

The kiss had meant everything to Willa. It meant he felt

something special for her. Mr. Long was a professional. He wouldn't do that if it didn't mean something—Would he?

She decided to try to get some information about him from the other teachers. She knew that she didn't fit in, that they hadn't really taken to her, but she occasionally joined them for lunch and now she decided to do so again. When his name came up she asked.

"Do you think he'll be back next year?"

"Well, why ever not?" Miss Applegate asked. He's doing a fine job. No reason not to come back. But what about you, Miss Arnott? Will you be back?"

"Why yes, I hope so—that is—unless—"

"Ah yes, a girl as pretty as you must have a beau somewhere just waiting. Of course, if Mr. Long finally marries his home town sweetheart they'll both move here, but no reason why he wouldn't continue as Principal now, is there?"

Willa Mae's heart just about stopped beating, but she was not about to let these women know. Somehow she got through the lunch, and soon rationalized that Mr. Long must not be serious about this other woman since he hadn't asked her to marry him yet. Besides, he had kissed her—Willa Mae Arnott, and he wouldn't have done that if he were serious about someone else. Willa was very sure that her Mr. Long was a superior man, with the highest virtues. He couldn't possibly be anything else, since he was the object of her affection.

Truth was, Willa Mae was not very experienced in the ways of the world, or of men. She was a very small town girl, whose social knowledge was based more on talk and gossip than on her own personal experience, and she had not had much education herself, even though she was a teacher. In fact, the idea of going back to school to study as Eva Jean was doing, was not what she wanted to do at all. What she wanted, was to marry this fine man, become the Principal's wife and then enjoy all the prestige, the fine living, and family life that she imagined would come with that title.

And so, in no time at all, Willa convinced herself that all

could still be well if only she could see the love of her life and straighten it out.

She was happy and carefree that next morning as she walked into the school. She would find him this very day, and she just knew once he saw her again it would all work out. Willa Mae was convinced now that he was being careful by ignoring her. She was sure it was his plan to protect her and once she had worked it all out in her mind, she was even more sure that her Mr. Long was her knight in shining armor.

"Morning Mrs. Applegate" she called cheerfully when she saw Mr. Long's assistant in the hallway.

"Look Willa Mae," Miss Applegate said as she joined her. She held out the local paper. "Mr. Long's engagement is announced. Isn't that something?" and Miss Applegate was off in a flutter.

She left Willa Mae standing speechless and stunned in middle of the hallway as students began to find their way into their classes.

Mr. Long had found the way to resolve the difficult situation with Miss Arnott all right. He had found the courage to propose to his long time girlfriend, his childhood sweetheart, and he was determined to move on with his life. Actually, he was rather pleased with himself. Certainly he was doing the honorable thing, and even he recognized that the delightful Miss Arnott had helped him make up his mind. His young girl friend had been waiting far more patiently than our Willa Mae could have imagined. and she was thrilled. Mr. Long had resolved it all quite satisfactorily, or so he thought. What Vernon did not realize was that he now had an enemy he didn't even know. He had never met, Mr. Milton Arnott, Willa Mae's father.

Chapter Twelve

The Twister

March 1913, Buffalo County, Nebraska

Looking back, Eva Jean realized that the storm hadn't really come so unexpectedly. As she'd walked to the school early in the morning, she'd noticed that the birds had stopped singing and the dawn sky seemed strange. There was no sun, but somehow the clouds had a yellow cast to them. The wind that they knew so well was quiet. In fact, there was no wind, but it was cold and very damp.

But she went about her chores, opening the school, lighting the coal stove with the bucket of coal she had set out yesterday afternoon, and cleaning the one blackboard. She'd tidied the classroom, straightening the seats and checking on the chalk supply. The students had all arrived on time, bundled up against the wind and the cold, and they had lined their school buckets up on the little wooden porch to keep their lunches cool and fresh. Three of her little group were absent with some kind of "chest". They had been coughing the day before, and she had told them to stay home and not make the others sick. She worried that they wouldn't miss too much.

It was ten o'clock before the wind really picked up. "Mizz Eva," little Lizzie Tanner called, "The lunches is blowin' around." They had all heard the rattle on the porch and Eva Jean scurried to the door and was shocked to have it flung back against the wooden building. "Joseph," she called "Get the buckets if you can. Don't leave the porch though. Just get what you can reach."

He lurched through the door, grabbed what he could and together they tugged as hard as they could at the door and finally slammed it shut. By then the wind was whistling through the chinks in the old school building. Sarah was crying.

"I don't like the wind," she said. "It's scary." And some of the others, the youngest, began to cry too.

All at once Eva Jean had a crisis on her hands because suddenly she knew just what was happening.

It was a twister. She remembered it just as it was when she was three, and her Daddy had held her so close, and had moved his whole family into the root cellar, just before it hit. They had lost the hen house, and the big garage. The house porch was gone, and part of the roof, but the rest was OK. It all came to her in an instant, particularly the fear that she had seen on her Daddy's face as he'd pushed his family, one by one, down the narrow stairs and pushed aside Mama's canned foods as he'd made room for them all.

Her heart was beating hard, but she couldn't let the children see how frightened she was.

"Hush now Lizzie. We're going to have a special vacation from our studies right this very minute."

"I wanna go home, Mizz Eva. I wanna go home!" It was Willie.

"Now Willie, you don't want to have to walk in these winds. We'll be safe all together."

She was tying a scarf around her waist as she talked. And she beckoned Joseph over and tied the end of it to his waist so they were securely tethered together.

"Joseph, we're going to have an adventure. You and I are going to open the coal bin. Boys and girls, don't be scared now, we're going where it's safe. The coal bin is underground, and we'll have to squeeze in but we'll make it."

"We'll get all dirty! Annie cried.

"I wanna' stay here!" yelled Lizzie, who grabbed onto Eva Jean and she had to pry her loose. "I wanna go home," wailed Willie.

"Willie, you stay right here now. Joseph and I will be right back. You all stay away from the windows. If the wind gets stronger it could break them."

She was all business now. She got them all onto the floor in the middle of the class and couldn't believe how strong she was as she moved the desks in a circle.

Just then, there was a terrific crack. They all froze as they knew it was the tree in the front of the school house, but there was no follow up sound of the crashing tree so she looked out the window and saw it horizontal on the ground, but moving past the school house like it was being pulled by a giant pulley.

That was it. She gathered their coats and told them all to put them on. There was no time for her and Joseph to go out, open the bin and come back for them. They would all have to go together. She had the key to the lock on her belt, and in a few minutes they each had on a coat and she did her best to tether them together. The strongest and biggest held onto the smaller children. She held Lizzie and Joseph held the squirming Willie.

"Lemme go!" Willie yelled. "Lemme Go!"

But Joseph bellowed at him.

"Shut yer trap ya' big baby. And hold tight."

They were out the door in an instant and the wind was horrific. They had to make it to the back of the schoolhouse, and she led them to the side she thought had the least wind. But there was no such thing. The wind seemed to blow from everywhere at once and they struggled step by step to make it. The little children had stopped crying and the bigger ones inched their way forward. They had just gotten to the doors of the bin when she realized that she couldn't open the lock while holding onto Lizzie. She pulled Clyde in front of her and made him kneel, then she laid

Lizzie down on his back, bent over Lizzie to protect her and free her hands. The lock held fast though the doors rattled, and she was terrified that she would drop the key, but it opened.

She almost pushed Clyde into the black coal lined pit. Lizzie shrieked.

"I don' wanna' go in there!" But the wind was so loud, they could hardly hear her and she was in anyway in a second.

How were they all going to fit in there? Joseph, bless his heart, knew she couldn't stand out there alone. Eva Jean was only 5'1" tall, and light as a biscuit. He was so fine and brave as he held onto her and helped all 9 children get into the cellar.

"Throw out the coal, heap it on you for weight. Make room, make room." Eva cried.

And the children, in a daze, did as she said. Joseph had dumped Willie inside as soon as he could, but Willie was terrified. They others were frightened too, but they didn't notice that Willie had a foot hold on a pile of coal. Just as Joseph was ready to throw Eva Jean on top of the heap and drop in himself, Willie bolted. One foot on the coal, the other on Arnold and he was out.

Eva Jean grabbed for him, but the wind took him away. She watched him stumble backwards, then saw the little boy rise into the air.

"Oh god, she cried!" Her voice disappeared in a moan with the wind. "Noooo!" But she saw him tumble in the sky, head over heels and then he was gone. He was simply blown away. It all happened so fast that none of the children saw it happen.

Joseph had her skirt and he yanked her back in as they managed to pull just one door on top of them. It held for a second, then was wrenched away. There was nothing to protect them, but they were all jammed in so tight they could hardly breathe. It was the only protection they had. Eva Jean was truly terrified, and as she screamed Willie's name the sound was simply carried away. The children never heard her.

They held their ears, they screamed back at the wind and ducked their heads. They called out to God to save them. There were sounds as things blew past them, all kinds of things, doors, a wash stand, a bicycle, wood, tremendous amounts of wood. Eva never saw part of the school roof coming at them but as it landed on top of their hiding place she felt it's smack and shake as it landed just over her head.

Would it ever end? Eva Jean could hardly breathe as big Joseph was on top of her. She had a fleeting thought of some of the children suffocating.

Then suddenly, the wind changed it's sound. It was dying down, and they could hear things dropping and hitting the ground with a crash or a tinkle or a bang. Joseph groaned as something large crashed on top of them and debris continued to rain down on them. And then, it was quiet. Very quiet.

Joseph moved first. He was OK. Then she heard the littlest ones wimpering just like they were babies again. But somehow she found her own voice. "Lizzie, is that you?" "Carrie? Clyde" One by one they answered yes. They were all alive, all scared and they all wanted out fast. But there was a huge pile of debris on top of them now, and although they could breathe, they couldn't move it. Joseph tried.

"Don't waste your strength Joseph, someone will come along soon." Eva Jean said. Sarah started to wail, the panic rising in her voice, and the others began to panic too.

She started to talk to them.

"Come on now. You're all right everybody. It's over and someone will be here in no time. Let's say the Lord's Prayer. Our Father"—and one by one they each joined in.

They didn't notice that Eva Jean stopped mid-way, her only thought for the little boy who wasn't there.

Then she began to sing and for some reason the only song that she could think of was "A Mighty Fortress is our God." Then Sarah joined in, then Cassie and soon they all sang as best they could.

Time began to drag. It could have been 15 minutes or an hour, and suddenly they heard sounds.

Actually, as soon as the winds dropped, townspeople had run to the schoolhouse. It hadn't been more than 10 minutes, but they were so stunned when they saw the schoolhouse gone that it took them several minutes to start to look around, and finally someone heard them.

Funny—they had all been so good really. The singing and the prayer had helped, but as soon as they knew they would soon be out, they all sort of panicked and some of them whimpered and cried and Eva Jean was just about to scream out loud herself, when there was chink of light, then another, and lo and behold, the last board was thrown off and they were out.

Eva Jean held each one of them, and kissed them until suddenly Sarah cried. "Willie, where's Willie?" She saw the tears washing down Eva Jean's blackened face and all at once each child knew that he was gone. But they couldn't scream—they were in shock from their experience, horrified by what they could not believe, that one of them had not survived. They clung together as their parents called their names, and ran to gather them up.

Suddenly, Willie's father stood there before her, his face bewildered, white. He knew even before he could form the words

"Where is he? Where is my Willie?" Eva Jean looked at his face, and fainted dead away.

March 16, 1913,

My Dear Thomas,

We are alive. My schoolhouse was lost, but my children were saved, all but one who got blown away in the big wind. I couldn't save him. I couldn't hold him, and I'll never forget him blowed away just like that. We hid in the coal cellar but he was scared and jumped out.

His Daddy blamed me at first. He said I shouldn't of let him out of the coal cellar, but when he saw that the whole school was gone and talked to the others, he said that he was sorry he'd blamed me. But oh, my sweetheart, I'll always blame me. Why couldn't I stop him? I loved him so, my little Willie who tried so hard and couldn't ever sit still for a minute. They found him a mile or so away at the base of a tree with his head on his arm just like he was sleeping. His back was broke from his neck to his knees. Oh, my Willie, my wee little boy!

I knowed what it was as I remembered that twister when we were kiddies. Do you remember? It sounded just like the trains going through, as if they was right on top of us. If my Daddy hadn't taken us into the root cellar then I wouldn't of thought of going to the coal cellar.

We were all so wrought up over it, that I couldn't start to teach again right away, so they gave us a few days and now we're all in a basement. It's dark and damp and we don't like it at all, but I do my best. It's very, very hard for the children. I didn't think I could go on at first, but Uncle Elroy said, "You have a job to do girl, go do it." so I did.

I'm so scared now, and I can't sleep. You know how I am with my handi—work,—it calms me down you could say, so I worked on our wedding quilt so fast I did two squares jiggety quick. Well Sir, you don't know how long it really takes, but two days is pretty quick work I tell you.

I think of you and long for us to be together. How I wish you were here now. Tell me it won't be long.

Affectionately,
Your Eva Jean

Chapter Thirteen

Life Goes On

Eva Jean was devastated by Willie's death. She could not sleep for seeing him lifted into the air over and over. She missed him terribly; his smile, his restlessness, his constant affection for her. She didn't know how she'd be able to go on, but it was expected. No sense fussing, no sense making too much of bad things. The funeral was solemn and sad and severe and grown up and the tears were quiet and dignified, except that Willie's mother couldn't hold back her moans and Eva Jean's hair stood up on the back of her neck when she heard it. Aunt Stella held her close then. Oh, yes, they were all there—the whole town. Mr. Anderson couldn't even speak to anyone. They—the family, would never be the same, but the rest of them were somehow expected to just get on with it.

"How am I going to do it, Auntie?" She walked the floors of their prairie house. She cried all night, and could barely find the energy to wash her face.

"I can't go back to them. I can't. We'll never be the same."

"Oh, my dear girl. Of course it will never be the same. You've all been through so much. But my dearest girl, life has changed for you before when you lost your mother and father. You came here to us and you made another life for yourself."

"But I was so young then. I didn't have a choice. I had to accept it. What could I do?"

Aunt Stella just held her then, and rocked her in her arms.

"Sshh," she said, as Eva Jean cried in her arms.

"Ssshh." It's the same now my dearest girl. It's the same now."

So they had a few days to gather themselves together. It was decided that the church was too cold to hold school all day, and Mr. Arnott offered the storeroom of his town general store. The coal stove was near the back wall of the store so it could warm the room behind it. For once, Eva Jean didn't have to do it all herself. Several of the men and women from town helped to stack boxes and make a space for them to work. She put up brown paper to write on, moved her own precious books into this makeshift school, and together, Eva and her little band of scholars started all over again.

She did her very best. When she saw that they couldn't concentrate any more, she'd read aloud to them. She tried to get them to sing, but they only remembered their singing in the coal pit and singing wasn't fun anymore. An essential part of who they were was gone, and they couldn't get over the loss. Finally, one day about two weeks later, she decided they just couldn't pretend any more. It was all too painful, and Willie was too much a part of them to be dismissed like this.

Her journal said:
The Journal:

Lord we all miss him so. Help me find a way to move us along and remember Willie too.

She had absolutely no idea how to go about facing their grief. She just thought of her own pain, and how she'd like to acknowledge Willie as a part of them all. How could she do it? For once, Aunt Stella couldn't help at all. She knew no other way than to keep going on. It was all the advice she had. But Eva Jean needed more, so late on Sunday long after the sun set, she asked Uncle Elroy to take her to church again and wait for her so she could just pray a little. She spent a little time alone in the cold and empty church. But when she left she felt no better.

When she climbed back up in the wagon, Elroy didn't say a word, just put his arm around her like he did when she was just a little girl and they drove home in silence.

She finally fell asleep early the next morning, but Aunt Stella called her in time to dress and get out the door in a hurry ready for school as always.

When the children arrived, she greeted each one of them at the store room door. Then she asked them to sit in a circle and she began.

"I'm really sad. Everyone wants us to go on about our work, but I think we need to talk about our friend, our Little Willie. I think we need to have something special for him but I don't know what to do. Does anyone have any idea?" There was a silence. No one knew what to say.

It was Anna who broke the silence. Big Anna was one of those who had missed school on that fateful day.

"Why don't we just write him a letter? We could write like he can see us. Pastor says he's in a safe place and he won't miss us; it's just us who miss him, so let's write him a letter and say so."

"Yeah," Joseph said "But what will we do with it?"

There was quiet while they all looked at one another. No one had an idea until finally Anna said, "We'll send it in the smoke from the coal stove."

"Anna. That's a fine idea. It will be a way for each of us to reach him. Thank you." And she reached out and took Anna's hand.

They spent the whole day then, talking about their lives in the little town, and how Willie was a part of it. They cried a lot, even Eva Jean, but then someone would tell a story and it was all right again. They took a break and Eva Jean read them a story from Mark Twain to take their minds off it all for awhile. By the end of the day, they had each written a letter. At school's end Eva Jean took Anna aside and thanked her again.

"You have helped us so much Anna. Someday you will be a wonderful teacher and a wonderful Mother too."

"Do you really think so, Miss Eva?"

"Yes, I really do. You're so smart and so creative. Look how excited everyone is about your idea. You've helped us so much."

Anna was truly glad to know she had been a help, that Eva Jean had liked her idea and that she thought she could be a good teacher, and even a good mother someday. That meant that there was someone who thought she could be married someday. Anna didn't believe anyone would ever want to marry her. Suddenly she had real hope for herself.

They each worked on their letters that night, and the next day, Eva Jean, asked each child to make one copy of the letter. Then they gathered around the coal stove in the front of the store. She had asked Reverend to come and say a prayer, which he did, and then they solemnly sent the letters to God and to Willie. Somehow they felt better then. She shook the Reverend's hand and thanked him. They all went back into the storeroom, and class continued as always.

That night, Eva Jean walked all the way to the Anderson's house with the copies of the letters.

"We—the class that is, just wanted you to have these. The children wrote their own stories about Willie, and someday you'll be able to read them. Maybe not yet," she added.

They invited her in but she didn't stay long. She accepted a hot cup of tea, and then Mr. Anderson drove her in the wagon, back to her home.

Eva Jean's letter: March 31, 1913

Dear Willie,

You were a good boy, and my favorite student, Willie, because I knew you couldn't help the restlessness. I know you felt so bad when people got mad at you for never sitting still, but I know you didn't do it on purpose. You moved around so much because you couldn't help it. But you were doing so well Willie. You were getting A in spelling. Did you know that? And your history was real nice and you counted right fine. You wrote good too, and I was so pleased that you took the time to form your letters so well. It was hard for you to sit, but you worked real good when I let you stand by my desk. I was going to get a special easel for you as you grew up so you could stand at it and write.

Remember when we talked that day when school began, when you and I sat together outside?. I put my arm around you just like I did when Mr. White used to yell at us. You would feel so bad then. But wasn't it fine that we had such a nice year together? Nobody yelled at you at all, and even Anna was learning how to help other kiddies. She helped you too, remember?

I will remember always. My sweet little boy-o who giggled as much as he wriggled.

God keep you Willie Anderson,
Your teacher,
Miss Eva Jean Carey

And the letters from Thomas

Dear Eva Jean,

I am so worried about you. Royal sent me a telly to tell me you were all right, but said that you would need me. It took two days for the fella in town to get the telly up here to me at the hogback. I'm working at the Dollerschell ranch now. They are good people and we all work hard. Our weather ain't so good either but we haven't had no twister. You take care now, and I'll call as soon as I can get to town.

Thomas

Dear Eva Jean

I just don't know what to say to you about all you been through. When I got your letter, I just sat and read it over and over. I feel so bad that you has to go through so much all by yourself. Such a little gal as you. I do remember the twister back when we was little, but it didn't come near our place. Now you been through two of them things. You were so smart to take them to the coal bin. Just think, what could a happened if you hadn't a done that. It was right smart, and I am so proud of you Eva Jean. Real proud. Now don't you go blamin yourself. You did all you could, and I know the town will understand. They are good people. Uncle Elroy is right. You can do it. You can go on, and I know you will. You seem to feel such a fondness for those kiddies. I don't know if that's a good thing, or bad. Makes it hard for you to care so much. Our roads is blocked good and I can't get out a here for while yet, but I'll come when I can. You keep going on now girl. You are my girl. You can do it.

Your Thomas

In the coming weeks, Eva did just go on. And her little band of kiddies went on too, doing their work and coming out of the dark storeroom every day glad to go home again. It was an even further walk for Eva Jean each day, so Mr. Arnott took the time to take her home himself, but she still walked there each morning alone.

The Journal:

My hope chest keeps me going. It has a few nice things in it that Aunt Stella got for me. I have made another waist for myself—a right nice one, all soft and pretty for my someday with Thomas. I hope there will be a time to wear it when we live on the farm. And I have two very nice aprons. Long ones with rick-rack on the bottom. I cheated a bit as Aunt Stella bought them and I put the rick—rack on by hand to make them special. We both crocheted four thick pot holders too, and Aunt Stella bought kitchen towels in a nice solid linen. She said they were the only kind to use on good glassware. I wonder when I'll have such a thing. And the quilt is coming along. I had to re-make one square that I did in such a hurry after the bad time when I didn't know what I was doing. I was real surprised to find I'd made such a mess. Slowed me a little, but it doesn't seem like Thomas and me can make plans soon so I suppose it doesn't matter.

Still not spring yet. Hope it will be soon. And can see my fellow. Thomas said I am "his girl." I feel so proud.

Chapter Fourteen

Spring

My Dear Thomas,

Our work goes on in our make-believe school-l room. But now that the prairie is coming alive to spring, it is better for us all. My kiddies brought me such a fine bouquet today. There were yellow lilies, larkspur, solomon flowers and even little cactus. It sure did brighten up our little school-room. Are there flowers on the hogback? Will I be able to pick them there? Does the meadow-lark sing? I don't know if I can live without the song of the meadow—lark every Spring. I miss you and only look forward to being with you again.

Your, Eva Jean

But still there was no visit from Mr. Johannson. He worked on a farm waiting for a reclamation on a barren expanse of treeless land. If there weren't others there to prove that the land was workable, it would be hard to believe. The roads were non-existent. Just ruts carved from the wagon wheels. He had fallen asleep once taking stores back from Sterling, and the horse had followed the wagon trail all the way to the door of the Dollerschell farm. Although it was too early to plant, there were livestock to care for, and it was impossible to get away. Still, he talked to Eva Jean once a month. They were careful with their words on the phone. They couldn't afford to whisper sweet nothings. Somebody was always listening in. They wrote often.

Dear Eva Jean,

The flowers here are just fine and real pretty too. They are busting all over now. I see you in my head, coming to our own little place with an armful of them. You will be a flower here yourself. We are working very hard, and I am making plans for us. But I want you to have a house even if it's awfully small at first. Do you think you can manage in a tiny place? I'll add to it as soon as I can, but we need a roof over our heads even if it's just a shed. It's too hard for couples to come here married with no place of their own. Then we'd each have to live with somebody else. When you come, I want us to be together. Be patient, my girl. Then we will always be together.

Yours, Thomas

Yes, there are meadow—larks. They surely do sound right fine. Now I'll think of you whenever I hear them.

Their letters sometimes took a long time to arrive and then they came two or three at a time. It wasn't like writing when you lived on the railroad line. Then, letters could get back and forth in a day.

This place was far from settled, but Thomas loved it already. It would make a good home for them both someday, and he wanted it to be just right when Eva Jean saw it for the first time. He had to have a place for them to live, and there had to be a well. It would take time, but he had high hopes that at the end of the summer he'd have his land staked out, and could start to plan. In the meantime, he was getting to know people as the community relied greatly on one another for help in building, for working the land, and certainly for friendship. He couldn't wait for Eva Jean to meet them. They were kind and friendly, and they gave new meaning to the words, "hard working." It was the difficulties that drew them together. In spite of it, they each held fast to a vision of developing this land, making their homes, farming, feeding a whole nation and someday passing it all onto their children.

As he stood on the hogback in the evening, watching the sun go down, he thought of her—of his girl.

"How I hope she'll love it here. She'll make us such a nice home and we'll have some kiddies of our own so she won't miss them scholars too much."

Thomas smiled to himself, remembering her. He hadn't seen her in so long, but although he couldn't remember her voice, he could still see her face, her soft little mouth and her smile and that wonderful hair of hers, curling all around her head. He missed her so terribly that sometimes he actually felt a pain inside his chest.

"Don't forget me—don't forget me" was his prayer.

In the meantime, Eva Jean was still struggling with her own grief. In order to keep their jobs, teachers had to be certified, and the superintendent of the district came regularly to check up on the teachers. The Institute would be giving classes to teachers to improve their knowledge and skills. There were two sessions. She could take four courses in all. But she worried about the expense and the time.

"But why should I spend the money? I'm going to marry Thomas and go be a wife and I already know how to run a house. I'm not going to teach forever you know."

But Aunt Stella thought it was just what she needed.

"Eva Jeannette, Thomas is nowhere near ready for you to go to Stoneham yet. It may be awhile, and this is just for a few weeks. You love to teach and besides, you need a change. This will do you good. Now you just get set and go."

And suddenly Eva Jean was very excited. She was going to study literature, and writing too. She'd meet other teachers and get all kinds of great ideas for her students. There was however, a big problem.

It was clear that the storeroom couldn't hold the whole school for next year with two more students added. The town fathers had decided they must build a new school. They wanted it to be of brick and they wanted a foundation that was poured and secure to protect their children. It would cost quite a bit but they all decided it was a necessity. So for the next year, the children would go by wagon to schools in surrounding towns. They could put the $600.00 that was Eva Jean's salary toward the new building. They wanted her back though. That was one good thing, she thought, if Thomas wasn't ready yet.

There were no openings in the schools close by, but up river was a small school in a community much like Elm Creek. It meant that she would have to leave her home with Aunt Stella and Uncle Elroy, and move into a stranger's home. Her salary would be smaller since room and board was part of her pay. She'd have to leave her precious hope chest behind of course. There would be no room. But now that she had a year of teaching behind her, Eva Jean thought she could do the job well.

Chapter Fifteen

Changes

It was Willa Mae who was in a very bad way. Far too embarrassed to leave her job, she was also humiliated to be there. But she found that she could cope. She did her work, was as pleasant as she could be to her fellow teachers, and as soon as she could leave for the day, she did. If anyone laughed at her behind her back she didn't know it. Vernon Long smiled, passed her by on the stairs, and never shared another private word with her. She thought he was disgusting now.

Just before the end of school, her parents visited, believing that they were going to meet their daughter's beau. Instead they learned that Mr. Long was to be married over the summer—to someone else.

Her Mother couldn't believe it. Somehow she was sure Willa Mae had spoiled her own chances.

"Whatever made you think this man wanted you? You were so sure of him, so sure he was the one."

"Oh, Mama," Willa Mae cried. "He lied to me. He told me he cared for me. I—I believed him."

Mr. Arnott was furious. "Did he lead you on girl? Is that what happened? Did he make promises to you?"

"Well, no Daddy, not exactly. He didn't promise me anything, but he spent a lot of time with me, and you can ask anybody, he never saw any of the other teachers alone. Just me. And—and—he kissed me."

That did it. Mr. Arnott was fit to be tied. "I'll have his job for this. Compromise my little girl will he? He'll find out you can't fool around with the Arnot's and get away with it. We'll sue him—that's what we'll do. We'll sue him for breach of promise."

Willa Mae was speechless. Her mother cautioned her husband.

"Now Harold take it slow. We don't want our girl to suffer any more."

"The man can't be allowed to get away with this; seducing young women and here he is in charge of young people. Well, he won't hurt my girl and get away with it. We'll take care of this right here in his own town and people will know just what kind of man this Long fella is."

Mr. Arnott spoke to a few people, made a few contacts and on the strength of his word alone, by the end of the day, Mr. Long was notified that he had better look for other work when the session ended. By the time Willa Mae was settled back at home, his engagement was ended as well.

The phone lines in Elm Creek had only just been restored after the tornado. Everyone had been so busy working to clean up the town that they hadn't much time to chat on phones, but now they started ringing before the Arnott's got off the return train. By that night every one in town knew that Willa Mae had ended her job, and had lost her beau. There were strong rumors that the fellow had been a cad. Could she have been "seduced?"

Aunt Stella's phone rang with the gossip while Eva Jean was at school. But Stella refused to believe all the talk and as soon as Eva Jean returned home her aunt urged her to call the Arnott's. Mrs. Arnott said that Willa was too upset to talk to her, but that she was grateful for her call.

In truth, Willa Mae was upset, but she was also ashamed that she had told Eva Jean about her romance. Now she couldn't fake her way out of it. She worked for hours on some story she could tell to cover herself, but she could only fall back on what she was convincing herself was the truth. Mr. Long had misrepresented himself. He had courted her in the privacy of the schoolhouse, had exacted a kiss from her—only one, but a passionate kiss nevertheless and had led her to believe that they would marry. His behavior was disgraceful, and her father was absolutely right to see that he did not have a position of responsibility with children. She was devastated to leave her precious schoolroom and the children she adored, but under the circumstances there was no way she could continue another minute. Her personal reputation was too precious to compromise in any way. She had called for her family to come to get her just as soon as she realized the kind of person he really was.

It was the story she was working on to cover herself. People didn't leave the classroom just before school ended unless they were ill. To do so was considered a great breach of trust. She'd see Eva Jean when she was more sure of herself, but not yet.

"Tell her I miss her, will you Mrs. Arnott? Tell her I can't wait to see her. It'll just be the two of us like old times." Eva said.

"I surely will dear," Mrs. Arnott replied. "She'll call."

But instead things took a turn.

The tiny notice of the Breach of Promise suit, appeared in the Kearney paper shortly after. It may have been a tiny notice, but so was the paper and it couldn't be missed. A friend even sent a copy to Royal knowing he had grown up in Elm Creek.

Mrs. Arnott contacted her sister in Denver, and before anyone was even aware, Willa Mae was on her way to stay with her aunt for an extended period. She and Eva Jean hadn't had a chance to get together at all.

The school ended in mid May, planting was underway and Uncle Elroy was taking Eva Jean to Chautauqua. She stopped in the new town to meet the people she would live with as an itinerant teacher, and was pleased to see that the house was comfortable and fairly large, although her own room was tiny and on the third floor that was really just an attic. There was just a bed and a wardrobe and a wash stand in the corner—no room for a table for her to plan her work.—No place to sit and do her needlework either. The lady of the house seemed a bit austere she thought, but Eva Jean was an optimist. It would be fine, she thought. She'd always made friends and she was sure she would do so here as well.

The school—room was very nice indeed with large boards to write on and a budget of $35.00 for supplies. She would have a much larger class of twenty-one scholars. That was a huge amount to teach all together in one room. For the first time since the twister she was excited and upbeat. She was going to learn wonderful things at Chautauqua for a new group of kiddies, and then she would be married. She wasn't sure how it would all fit together but she told herself all her new skills would make her a better wife and mother.

Dear Thomas,

I love it here. It is very hot but we study in the early morning so we can rest in the afternoon. We read wonderful books and I am learning much about Mark Twain. I didn't know half of what he wrote. We are also studying works by Charles Dickens and it is a thrill. And Thomas, you won't believe it, but I am learning about Shakespeare. I couldn't even read it at first. It was too hard and didn't make any sense. But they had a traveling company of players perform for us, and now I can understand what it's all about. I had never seen a play before. Oh, Thomas it is really quite wonderful! We saw Midsummer Nights Dream. I hope to be able to do a few scenes with my students next year. I hope to get a good certificate and be able to teach a good school.

I have little time, but I still work on my handiwork when I can. There is gaslight here. It's built right into the walls. It is wonderful to have light to study by at night. Do you think we will have it at the farm someday?

I so hope you aren't working too hard during the season. I know I can't see you, but when all is planted, won't you have some time before the harvest?
Take care of yourself, Thomas,

Your girl,
Eva Jean

Dear Eva Jean,

It sounds like you are hard at work. I am disappointed that you couldn't come to see us here at Stoneham. I thought you would have some time before you had to get to that institute. Could Royal bring you up before you teach? I have a nice place for you to stay with a fine family I've gotten to know. They have a daughter, Thea, just your age. She's a nice girl. You can stay with them and Royal can bunk with me. I know your schooling is important to you. Don't get too fancy for me now will you? It sounds as if you are learning a whole lot of things I don't know much about. Shakspear ! Well that's pretty fancy for sure.
How many fella's are there Eva Jean? I hope they're all ugly. Ha Ha—That's my joke.

Your fella
Thomas

Chapter Sixteen

Buffalo Bill And
The Wild West Show

Eva Jean worked so hard at her lessons at Institute that summer of 1913 that she didn't spend much time with others. She was quiet and stayed by herself a lot. But she had her friends who knew her from the summer before, and knew she had lost a student to the storm, and that she missed her beau. They respected her privacy, but saw to it that she wasn't alone too much of the time. Eva Jean was grateful. Still she looked forward to seeing her brother again. At least that would be a comfort and they would have fun for two whole days.

The whole institute was abuzz with the news that the famous Wild-West show was to be in Lincoln during their sessions. They planned to go in a group, and Royal was to join them.

He arrived late one morning.

"Hi ya', Sister! How's my girl?" Eva Jean had just come out of class and she threw herself in his arms as she always did. But there were strangers there, so she caught herself almost at once and backed off just a little. But Royal was so glad to see her too, that he gave her a big hug anyway. Introductions were made and arm in arm, they walked away to spend the afternoon talking almost non-stop about everything.

The Wild West Show was everything they thought it would be. People came for many miles around to see it. It was better than a circus because it was of and from the West itself. Buffalo Bill was their hero. He had dined with Kings and Queens and brought respect to the hard land and its people. It was loud and boisterous, a drum banging, hootin', hollerin', shootin' laugh out loud, oohh'n and ahh'n evening of terrific fun.

They all drank root beer, and ate big sausages, cheered as the Indians attacked. The horses were particularly beautiful. They were groomed and shining and unlike the work-horses back home, they actually performed as if they had a brain and could understand human instructions.

But then, there was Buffalo Bill himself. He sat tall in the saddle, and he looked fine and proud. It was a wonderful night, and Eva Jean laughed and held onto Royal like he was her lifeline. She forgot her reserve and the two of them held hands or Royal had his arm around her shoulder. When the Indians came out shooting and hollering, Eva cringed behind Royal's back and he pulled her head down on his shoulder as if he were protecting her, even though they both were laughing.

"Who cares what anyone thinks," Eva Jean decided boldly. "He's my brother, so what?" She just decided to have a good time and stop worrying about anyone else. Perhaps for the first time in her life Eva Jean thought. "I deserve this—I deserve to just have a good time. Yes, indeed, I do."

It was more than a week later that back in Elm Creek, Aunt Stella met up with the mother of one of Eva Jean's former students.

"Well now, we here tell that Eva Jeannette will be giving up her teaching soon. Going to get married we hear."

Aunt Stella was surprised that Mrs. Tanner would mention it. "We all hope so, but it won't be soon. Thomas is trying to get a piece of land through reclamation in Colorado, and then he wants to build a small house for them first."

And then Mrs. Tanner said the strangest thing.

"Oh, we hear that it isn't Thomas at all. "S'posed to be a new fella. Someone she met at this fancy school she's in. They've been seen mighty lovey-dovey. Now you know I'd never say a word against Eva Jean, but I just thought things had changed for her. After all that Thomas boy has been gone a long time now."

"Why no—no, that can't be. We'd know. I'm sure you're wrong, Mrs. Tanner."

But Stella wasn't sure. Had something happened that Eva Jean hadn't mentioned? If so, she were sure Eva Jean would call. She had no way of reaching her by phone. In the first place she wouldn't know how to place a long distance call, and she wouldn't know how to reach Eva Jean if she could get through. But if it were anything, Eva would let them know, she was sure of that.

No news came in the post in the next few days, so Stella wrote.

Dearest Girl,

> *I heard tell that you have a new fella? Is that right? I need to know what to tell people.*

> *Love, Aunt Stella*

and several more days before she got a reply.

Dear Aunt Stella,

> *Why, whatever do you mean—a new fellow? Of course not. My fellow is now and always will be, Thomas Johannson. Don't let anyone tell you any different. Who says?*

> *Your niece, Eva Jean*

At first she didn't pay it any mind at all.

"What nonsense!" she thought.

But then she got to thinking that if a rumor could get all the way to her Aunt, maybe it could get to Thomas, too.

"Oh, but that's silly, he's so far away"
Still, she wrote him a letter so he'd know the truth.

Journal:

Wrote Thomas that if he hears a rumor about me and someone else, it isn't true and I don't know how it got started. I said, "Are you still my fellow? Because I am still your girl." Hope he won't worry when he gets it. If it was him with the rumor, I'd likely think something was going on somewhere. But it sure isn't here.

The day she posted the letter the storms began. They swept the plains causing massive flooding all over. Parts of the railroad tracks were washed away, and no mails could be delivered for weeks. When they did start to move again, many bags of mail had been damaged by the water and were undeliverable including all of Eva's remaining letters.

The rains brought further disappointment to Eva Jean who has so looked forward to seeing her beau again. It had been all planned. She and Aunt Stella were going to Colorado. There wouldn't be time to go up to the land, but they would meet Thomas in Sterling and the three of them would visit. Now her chance to see him again was gone. Not only could they not go, but there was no way to even send a telegram. They just guessed that he would know. Truth was Thomas had no way to get out of Colorado either.

So the rumor had died down by then. Aunt Stella and Uncle Elroy, Eva Jean herself and Royal told everyone they knew that Thomas and Evie would be married someday, and Eva Jean stopped worrying. It was all over.

Chapter Seventeen

The Denver Deb

This is the life. Willa Mae was bouncing back nicely from her sad disappointment over Mr. Long. Denver was a dream come true. Already a real city with a character of its own, Willa Mae found it thrilling. Her aunt was a part of a growing group of well—to—do people that were going to make Denver an important spot in America. She knew everyone in town including the now famous Molly Brown, survivor of the Titanic. Her aunt said that Molly Brown had been ignored by all of Denver society until the tragedy, but now people couldn't get enough of her. Willa Mae was in the right place in the right time.

Mrs. Arnott had been jealous of her sister for years. They had each inherited a nice amount from their grandfather who was one of the few who had panned for gold in '49 who had actually made a fortune. Mrs. Arnott, had married and put her money into her husband's hands and had no real wealth of her own. But her sister had maintained control of her own fortune; never marrying, never having children, but instead investing well and reaping the rewards.

"But of course," Mrs. Arnott, told herself. "I have my Willa Mae, and I won't let my sister get my hands on her. She's my gold." Although the sisters had stayed in touch, the Arnott's seldom visited Denver, and when they did, Willa Mae was never allowed to spend as much as an hour alone with her aunt.

Now, of course, everything was changed. Mrs. Arnott needed her sister Hazel to help her out, and Hazel was more than glad to do so. Once she made sure the girl hadn't really been compromised in any way, she welcomed her. Willa Mae was pretty and Hazel believed she'd have fun showing her around and introducing her to her friends.

For her part, Willa Mae was thrilled with the opportunity. She was finally living a life she had only dreamed about. She shared the large house with her Aunt and several servants. Imagine, servants!—and she had one to help her with anything she wanted to do. She was taking music lessons too, playing the piano,—badly, and singing—not so badly. In fact Willa Mae had a rather pretty voice.

She had written to Eva Jean just as Thomas had, and like him, her letters were washed away in the rain. Her aunt saw to it that she could talk to her mother every two weeks, although they had to arrange for a telephone where the lines hadn't been torn down. Actually, Mrs. Arnott traveled South about ten miles and waited at a little store owned by her husband. The phone lines were terrible. They crackled and hummed and sometimes she could hardly hear.

"How's Eva Jean?" she had almost shouted to her Mother one day in late August.

"All right I guess." Her mother shouted back. "They're saying she's met someone new."

"What?—What?"

The line hissed and sizzled. "—going to be married in spring.—someone else—they were seen in Lincoln together"

"Who?—Eva?—Mother—Mother?"

But the line died just as her mother tried to tell her she didn't believe it a bit. Must be just a rumor.

"Well imagine that!" Willa Mae said to herself. "Eva, with another fella" and the jealousy returned in an instant.

"She has two, and I don't even have one! The very idea!" Willa Mae was not unlike her own mother.

But the most important thing was to have some fun.

"I'll find me a beau in no time, and he won't be any farmer or a teacher either."

So—first things first. Find some friends. And she did.

It didn't take long either. The singing lessons led to some performing for her aunt's friends, who introduced her to their young daughters, who took her to dancing school where she met some nice young men.

Then an opportunity for an adventure came up suddenly. A new friend, Nettie Teppel, was to travel with her parents to a place called Cheyenne, Wyoming. Her father would do some business with livestock and they would all attend a rodeo that had gained in popularity and was known as one of the best of the small town events. It was Cheyenne Frontier Days, and they would see bronco bustin', hog tyin', and bull doggin'. There was also a special treat that year. A girl cowboy, the first they would ever see was to compete against the men. Bertha Kaepernik was supposed to be one darned-good rider, so they said. Nettie invited Willa Mae to join them.

At first, Willa Mae wasn't too sure. She'd seen her share of rodeos as a prairie child. It was just about the only event that was common on the prairie. Cowboys took the skills that they used everyday in their jobs and made a competition out of it. It was fun for them to establish some kind of expertise and many had gone on to join circuits of rodeos that traveled around all the small towns and performed. It was a kind of show-business of the prairies. But it didn't have the glamour of a Wild West show like Buffalo Bill's. So Willa had to think for a minute.

"Come on Willa Mae, can you imagine some girl in knickers riding a horse and competing in bronco busting? It'll be fun, you'll see. Besides, we're going to go by train." Nettie urged.

Nettie was beautiful, and she was well known, and had many friends and she was inviting Willa Mae.

"A girl cowboy—competing yet. She must be ugly. I've got to see." So it was all set, and in early September, Willa Mae with her new friends set off to see something new and exciting, a fitting event for a girl of the prairies, and one who sought to get ahead.

It was all that she could have imagined. The town was just another old dusty dry, wooden jerkwater like all the others, but it was a big week, with many people from all over, and they stayed in a real hotel. Willa Mae and Nettie walked that dusty old street in their finest white linen tucked dresses and their high polished boots with their hair pulled back neatly, and they flirted with those dirty old cowboys who hadn't seen anything quite like these Denver misses. The giggled and they whispered and they had a fine time.

The rodeo was swell too, and Miss Bertha Kaepernik was a wonder. She rode a horse like no man had ever seen. Rode him to a standstill as a matter of fact, and the whole crowd stood up and cheered. The newspaper reported that:

"The crowd cheered themselves weak at the sight of a woman riding as they had not conceived that a woman could ride."

Much to Willa Mae's surprise, she wasn't ugly at all. It was a thrill that Willa Mae would not soon forget.

Across the arena, Thomas, his boss Mr. Dollerschell and his daughter Althea screamed along with the rest. Suddenly he saw her. That pretty miss with the fancy dress and the shiny black hair could only be Miss Arnott.

"Meet ya' at the gate. I see someone, I got to talk to." And he was gone before they could even ask him who it was.

Thomas' heart was beating like a hammer. Willa Mae would know. She'd get a message through to Eva Jean, he just knew it. It had been since early July since he'd had a letter. There had been the storms, and then weeks to repair the railroad, and there were no phones anywhere in Weld County. Then, when he'd tried to get to her, the crops were ready and he couldn't go. He had tried to reach Royal at one of his trips to a town that had a telegraph, but Royal had been moved to another station, and he couldn't find him.

Finally, through the crowd he saw her.

"Somebody's calling you Willa Mae."

"Who on earth?"

And there he was beside her. He was dirty and unshaven,

and at first Willa Mae didn't have any idea who it was, but then suddenly she realized it was Thomas—

"Willa tell me about Eva Jean. Have you heard anything? I can't reach her." He looked so worried that Willa Mae was sure he had heard it too.

"Just that she's to be married next Spring—Some fella'she met at Institute I guess. It was all over town. I'm sure sorry Thomas"—

Thomas was so stunned he couldn't move. He couldn't even talk.

But Willa chattered on.

"I heard you're going to get a reclamation. How's that going? You must work pretty hard out here. I live with my aunt in Denver now, so I don't see anybody back home anymore. Not often anyway."

"Married"—he finally blurted out.

"Well now, you're a sod buster Mr. Johannson. Good luck to you. You need a good farm wife, not a working girl like Eva Jean."

"Come on Willa Mae" urged Nettie. "Daddy's waiting."

"Got to go now, Good luck to you Mr. Johannson." And she fairly sashayed away.

Thomas watched as she linked arm and arm with her friend and they sauntered off into the distance.

He couldn't move. He couldn't believe it.

"Thomas, Thomas are you alright?" It was Althea Dollerschell. She was right be his side in a minute, and he let himself be led away, his head a jumble.

To be fair, Willa Mae really did give it a second thought.

"You don't suppose he didn't really know," she thought. She remembered her mother saying something at the end of their phone call that sounded like—"just a rumor, or don't believe it."

But there was Miss Bertha the bronco-buster greeting the crowd. In a wink Willa Mae forgot all problems as she too crowded nearer to get a glimpse up close of her new heroine.

Thomas wanted, needed to talk to her again. "I'll find her," he thought. "This is impossible." But the crowd swirled around him too and his boss was at his side, and he was led in the other direction as they prepared for the long ride back to Stoneham.

All of the letters of reassurance that Eva sent remained undelivered. She started her new job in a new place and wrote again. The roads were repaired and then rains came again. More wash outs—more delays. Then the rains turned to hail and by October the snow was starting for what would be the worst winter in years.

Eva Jean waited. There was nothing more she could do. She couldn't leave her school to travel to him. Even the telegraph lines were down again. Her birthday passed and not a word.

And then:

Journal entry, October 26, 1913

"I'm real scared. There was some kind of rumor going around last summer that I've got a new boyfriend, though nobody can put a name to him. It was awhile ago and I thought it was all past. I haven't heard a word from Thomas. Not a word. I haven't seen him since January, but our letters kept us close. He's everything to me, all my hopes and dreams. What is wrong?"

111

Chapter Eighteen

Prairie Strong

It was November when she finally went home for a visit and Royal was there too. Royal was doing very well in the telegraphy field. He was a trainer now for Western Union and he traveled from place to place. He showed her the notice at dinner when Aunt Stella and Uncle Elroy were there. He'd already prepared Stella.

The notice he'd been sent was a simple announcement from the Sterling Post.

Miss Althea Dollerschell of Sterling was to be married on December 15, to Mr. Thomas Johannson of Grand Island, Nebraska. She was the daughter of Mr. and Mrs. Clyde Dollerschell. Mr. Johannson was a new homesteader and they would make their home on his recently claimed land, his 160 acres next to that of the Dollerschells.

December 15 was three weeks away.

"Tell me what to do Eva Jean. I know this is crazy. He loves you, I know he does. I'll go there. I'll find him and stop this. It's a mistake."

Eva Jean was in shock. She read the notice over and over again. Somehow it was a dream. The words didn't really say that, did they? Thomas, her Thomas marrying someone else—someone named Althea. Where had she heard that name? Why, that was the girl she was supposed to stay with when she went to him. And now he's going to marry her?

But it was just a few months ago that she expected to see him. How could this be happening?

The family just sat there and looked at her. Uncle Elroy reached out and took Stella by the hand. Eva Jean got up from the table, looking dazed.

"Excuse me," she said. "I'd, I'd like to be alone for awhile."

At the table they talked quietly about it, then Stella sent Royal up to her.

He found her sitting at the hope chest sorting through her things. She had laid it all out in little piles on the floor all around the lovely, polished box. There were the blouses she had made for herself, the waists as she called them, the anti macassers she and Aunt Stella had crocheted for the nice stuffed furniture she'd have someday. There were the kitchen linens, the aprons with the rickrack and the embroidery cloth she'd just finished last summer. Only one napkin remained unfinished. She was just reaching the quilt, as it lay on the bottom of the box when Royal walked in and sat down next to her.

"It's great stuff, Eva Jean. It's all beautiful. You'll use it I know you will."

She smiled at him.

"I think I'll take the waists back to school with me. They're a little fancy but they should be worn. I have a student who can wear them, I'm sure she can, and she'd love them, I know. Can't keep 'em forever you know. Styles change."

"Eva Jean, I'll take some time off and go up there to see him. It's just so—"

"Ssshhh," she said. And she put her finger on his lips.

"Hush now. No point in that. There's plans all made and Thomas isn't stupid, he knows what he's doing. I haven't seen him in so long—I don't even have his picture. He was just about your height wasn't he, Royal, Just about that tall? Maybe that's why I liked him so much. He was just like you.—Lucky girl this—Thea." She choked on the name, but still no tears.

The light from the lamp glowed warm and wan across the little room. Royal sat with her while she fingered all her things, then carefully laid them back in the box. He thought that she would break when she picked up the quilt. How many hours had he seen her sit with those squares in her hands, each stitch, one by one—their wedding quilt. But she folded it so lovingly, and kissed it and placed it gently on top, then closed the box.

Royal was just getting up, feeling stiff from sitting so long on the floor beside her, when she picked up the journals and the letters cascaded to the floor. All of his letters, his hand the only thing she'd had all these months, just his handwriting to sit and touch and to dream about and remember the kisses.

Aunt Stella heard her moan all the way in the kitchen. When she got upstairs Royal was holding her and she was screaming— not a scream exactly, but a keening sound like Mrs. Anderson had made at Willie's funeral, a sound so awful and unreal that Royal was terrified by it—this noise coming out of his sister.

They put her to bed then, and Aunt Stella stayed until she couldn't cry any longer and was asleep at last.

"I swear if I ever see him again, I'll kill him."

"For heavens sake boy, I don't want to hear that kind of talk in my house. It just wasn't meant to be. That's all there is to it. She's not even twenty yet. She'll get over it, and she's got her job and all. Eva Jean isn't a doll baby like that Willa Mae. She can cope all right. She just has to get through this part. She's going to be all right I tell you."

Chapter Nineteen

Surviving

And Aunt Stella was right. She was all right. The next morning, she got up and went to church same as always. She talked to Mrs. Arnot and heard all about Willa Mae living with her Aunt in Denver. Her friends didn't think she looked so good. "A bit peaked" was how they put it. She came home, but instead of baking all afternoon with Aunt Stella, she sat in a chair staring out the window. But then she packed some clean clothes, took the hand made waists with her, and Uncle Elroy drove her in the new truck all the way back to her new residence.

Once back at school, she plowed into her schoolwork.

"I'd like you to have these, Kate, she said, as she gave the blouses to her student. I made them myself and can't wear them. They're too nice for school but I'm sure you'll like them for church."

Kate was absolutely thrilled and her family totally puzzled.

Eva Jean was the same as always; or at least it seemed that way as long as she was working, either at school or doing the million and one jobs that her landlady, Mrs. Austin, dreamed up for her to do. On her day off, she was expected to do the laundry, a job that took three days to finish. She was also to sweep every morning before she left their house at 7:00 a.m. and she was expected to help with dinners as well. They used her like a hired girl, and she wrote in her journal that she was "tired to the death"

She was all right, just fine, you could say, except that she cried herself to sleep every night, couldn't eat and was rapidly losing weight. It wasn't long before she was ill. She got up same as always, walked to the school in the cold, opened it and fired up the stove.

Then one morning the scholars found her on the floor when they got there and she was taken back to her room in a wagon. The doctor was called and he was not happy with the state of her health or with the tiny room she lived in on the third floor.

"Mrs. Austin, you've got a large room downstairs. This girl isn't a maid, she needs room to do her work and relax in. She can't stay in this room now. The stairs are too hard for her."

"She never complained," Mrs. Austin said. "I thought she was all right."

Once she could talk again, and the doctor realized that she had been overworked here in this house, he decided that she must move as soon as possible. He and his wife had a nice large house behind his surgery and his daughter's room was still there. So they packed her up and moved her in as soon as she was well enough.

And with a cheerful place to live, and warmth from large fireplaces and a good stove, and a place to move around, Eva Jean began to mend. Mrs. Kenny, the Doctor's wife, was happy to have a young woman around the house again, but she didn't quite know what to make of this girl, who was so wan and sweet, but seldom smiled. Still, she was willing to give her her own time and she didn't push.

The Journal, December 1913

So different this year. I can see them looking at me to see if I'm all right now. Part of what makes it so hard is that I don't know. If I could only know what happened, maybe I wouldn't feel so let down. If I'd seen him long enough for us to disagree on something, or to get mad at one another, it would be easier somehow—I think.

My students are so different. I knew the others so well from home, but these children are new to me. I'm still trying to get to know them all as individuals. I have four different levels to teach now. It's hard, but Mrs. Kenny gives me time to do my school work. She is so much nicer than Mrs. Austin who was really an old biddy. I know Mrs. Kenny thinks something's wrong with me, but she is kind anyway. After Christmas I'm going to do a play with the children. I think we'll offer it to the church for a fund-raiser. Might be fun for a change. I really am an old maid. I forgot what fun is!

It took time. January,—February passed. Eva Jean was eating fine now, enjoying the pleasantness of life with the Kennys, but working incredibly hard at her job. She had the play to work on. They were doing the wall scene from Midsummer Nights Dream and the children were having a wonderful time. They presented it to the parents who liked it so much they asked Eva to direct the adults in a play for the Spring, so she was hard at work trying to find the right thing to do. And then she found it. It was called, The Drunkard, or the Fallen Saved, by William Gillette, and it was a real melodrama. They could have fun being dramatic.

But the good doctor watched her to see that her weight was all right. She kept saying that she felt fine. And in truth she was working so constantly that she didn't think too much about anything else. The work kept her going. And then she saw the letter.

The letter went to Aunt Stella's of course, so she didn't get to see it until late March when she went home. They were almost sorry to give it to her. She was looking so much better, Aunt Stella was afraid that she'd fall apart again. But she didn't. Eva Jean read it, cried a bit, then shared it with them all.

Dear Eva Jeannette,

I talked it over real good with Thea, and she said we should write to you so you can understand. Last week I bumped into your brother Royal in Denver where he's teaching for Western Union I guess. He wasn't very happy to see me, let me tell you, and I was lucky not to get a punch in the nose. Can't say I blame him.

Eva Jean, I thought you was going to be married. It was Willa Mae who told me. I ran into her in Cheyenne. She is your best friend. Why would Willa Mae tell me a made up story? Anyway's I tried to get to see you but you know the storms spoiled that. I was just about crazy over it all but Thea was here and she helped me get through it. She's a real nice girl, and you would like her, I know you would. She knows all about you and that's why she's helping me write to you. I don't spell so good you know.

Royal says you are a wonderful teacher and that you are all right. I'm so glad because I near died when he told me it was all a lie. But at the same time, I am so happy with Thea, and we are going to have a kiddie of our own soon, that I do feel that things is meant to be. I'm sorry about everything, except that Thea and I are very happy, and I'm not sorry it turned out this way after all.

I will always wish you the very best.
Your friend, Thomas

Underneath in another handwriting it said,

It really was awful hard for him, but he's real fine now. I want to make him happy as he is a good man. Thea

Eva Jean turned to her brother and said.

"Roy if you meet up with Willa Mae in Denver, you can punch HER in the nose for me."

And for once, Aunt Stella didn't say a word.

Chapter Twenty

Critters

Willa Mae had been away for some time now. She heard about the break-up of her old friend's romance, but never considered for a minute that she might have had something to do with it. In fact, Willa Mae was glad to know that she wasn't the only one who had a broken romance.

In a way, she felt that she and Eva Jean were at last alike. She didn't have to envy her anymore. Eva Jean wasn't so perfect as her mother always said she was. Oh, she was still a teacher, and she had her certificate, and was working on a real college degree, but still, Miss Goody, Two Shoes, Eva Jeannette, had suffered just like Willa Mae had suffered.

Her new friends kept her busy and she loved her new dresses which she'd had to get because she ate such wonderful foods she needed new clothes. Her mother had persuaded her father to drop the suit. For one thing there was no one to corroborate Willa Mae's story of promises and kisses, and for another Mr. Long hadn't given her a ring or any other pledge. Keeping it going would only bring more notoriety to their family. Mr. Arnott had succeeded in his main aim. Mr. Long was no longer employed in education, but had moved East to Chicago.

But it would soon be Easter, so Willa Mae had made the trip back to Elm Creek. She had been picked up at the station by her father in the new car. She'd settled back into her own room at home but in no time, she was bored and decided to dress up special to give her old friends something to see. She picked her green and white striped waist, her long green skirt and jacket and walked into town to see who was still around. From the whistle of the 2:00, she pretty much knew just who would be in town, and where they would be. She'd stop by to see old Mr. Jackson at the general, and see who else was there. Mrs. Tanner, Sarah's mother would surely be at the post office as always.

But it was the strangest thing. No one in particular cared to talk to her. The warm and friendly greeting she expected wasn't there. They didn't seem to have much time for her. Mrs. Tanner didn't even smile and rushed away without much of a greeting at all. Nelson at the telegraph became very busy with papers on his desk when she bounced in to see him and tried to get him to reminisce. Why, he didn't pay her no mind at all. What was the matter with everybody? They seemed to brush her off, and turn away, not at all intrigued by her pretty dress, or her toss of her curls, or her dimples. Willa Mae was annoyed.

"My goodness, has everyone forgotten me already?"

The truth was simply that everyone knew that it was Willa Mae who was responsible for bringing so much pain to their favorite friend, neighbor, and teacher, Miss Eva Jeannette Carey. Too polite to insult her directly, they nevertheless quietly conveyed to her their complete lack of interest in anything she had to say, or do. Willa Mae was puzzled, annoyed, and finally angry.

"Well, I see this little old town has really become so boring there isn't any point to visiting at all."

She pulled her jacket around her, swished her skirts behind her and flounced out of the telegraph office determined to get home as quickly as she could. Willa was an optimist. She was sure Sunday would be different. Sunday she would go to church wearing her nicest dress and she'd turn their heads then for sure.

She headed back up the road. It was a warm day, and she took off her jacket as she went.

Back at the telegraph, the new telegrapher shook his head as he read the latest news reports. There was a swarm of grasshoppers heading their way. He sent the news as fast as he could to outlying towns, and hoped that it would travel to the farms. Not that there was much that anyone could do.

At just about that time, Eva Jean and Aunt Stella were out in back hanging up the laundry. She was home for a short time, and Aunt Stella hated to put her to work,but as usual Eva Jean herself had said she wanted to help. It was always nice to be outside doing this particular woman's work with her beloved Aunt. They would chat and sometimes share news—well, it was gossip is what it was, but they would just enjoy being together and chatting about whatever.

They heard the sound from far away. It was a humming, or was it a buzz? And then they saw the sun seemed to dim.

Stella was the first to realize what it was.

"Oh, my! Oh my, it's the hoppers! We'd better get down what we can girl. Help, quick now." and one two three, she was tearing at the clothes to pull them off the lines as fast as she could.

Eva Jean didn't ask questions. She joined her and together they pulled down what they could and started back to the house with the laundry basket between them.

They made it to the back door just as the first of the hoppers hit. They dragged the basket in and slammed the door, slapping the critters as they made it through the door.

Willa Mae didn't get half way home before she heard the noise. She hadn't any idea what it was from. She just stood at the side of the road looking around, wondering what was that awful racket? The truck came out of nowhere. It pulled up just ahead of her, and a voice yelled.

"You'd better get in here, or you'll be sorry."

Royal hadn't really seen the girl, just knew he should get her out of there. He was too busy looking behind him to see if the hoppers were upon them yet when she got into the car, and he pulled away fast.

They bumped along for several long minutes, while he said "Those locusts will eat everything in sight—Where you going, I'll drive you there. Just hope it's not far."

"Why Royal for heavens sake, it's me. It's Willa Mae."

He was so shocked he turned, slammed on the brakes and skidded to a stop.

"You!" he said.

"Well, yes, it's me."

"How can you even think of getting in my car after what you've done?"

"What are talking about? Willa Mae was getting scared and her voice was small and shaky when she said.

"What did I do?"

He couldn't just sit there. The cloud was getting closer and so was the noise. Royal started the car and they careened off down the road.

"Darn you Willa Mae, you just about ruined my sister's life, that's what. You told Thomas that she was marrying someone else. And he believed you—why wouldn't he? And so he married someone else. You—you no good little—

Willa Mae held on to the car door for dear life. Royal was so mad he was driving crazy. Only part of it was to get away from the critters. The other part of it was to scare the bejeezus out of Willa Mae. He succeeded.

She started to cry and yell.

"I didn't mean any harm. Everybody was talking about it. He didn't have to believe me."

They were just about a quarter of a mile away from the Arnott's house. He could drive her there and up the long driveway and stay with them. On the other hand if Royal drove like crazy, he'd likely make it home to Aunt Stella's just in time. Maybe.

It wasn't hard to decide just what to do.

He slammed on the brakes.

"Get out!"

"What?—Royal you can't!"

"Oh yes I can. Run like hell and you'll make it before they land., and if you don't, I don't care"

He reached over and opened the door. One look at his face and Willa Mae was more afraid of him than of the noise. She jumped out and he slammed the door.

"Run!" he screamed.

He was off. In the window he could see her running and the critters just behind her. He saw her start to fight them off just before he sped away.

Willa Mae did run like the dickens, and she made it home all right, but not before the hoppers ate the green stripes off her dress, and munched a few bites out of her as well. She fought them off, and tripped on her disintegrating dress, but she made it home with the blouse in tatters and only her knickers left where the skirt had been.

At just about that time Stella and Eva Jean were also making it to their house. The difference was that they managed to watch in amazement and even with some laughter at the critters as they landed on everything green in sight. They were safe inside. Willa Mae got to see them close up and intimate. She arrived home hysterical, and had to be put to bed.

When Royal arrived and told them his story, Aunt Stella started to frown.

"Boy, you don't mean to tell me that you let that girl out in a storm of locusts? Why, what was you thinking? Where's your Christian manners?" But her frown turned to a little smile, and in spite of herself she started to laugh. Eva Jean was trying not to hide a giggle, but when she saw Aunt Stella laugh she couldn't help herself.

Royal said, "Why it's positively Biblical!" all three of them broke down. Eva Jean laughed so hard the tears ran down her face. But they remained tears of laughter.

Journal, April 1914

I laughed today. It was the first time I've laughed out loud in a long time. Royal was the cause of it. I surely won't ever forget why I laughed and as long as I live I hope I never stop laughing again. It has been a long hard time since my life changed so.

Chapter Twenty One

New Lives

Down in Colorado, in the vast, endless prairies, Thomas made a new life with his young bride at his side. Together, in the midst of the vast prairie, with only a rutted path outside their door, they built a tiny shack, and set up a home by themselves. It stood alone, not a tree or a shrub nearby; but at night, when a single kerosene lamp lit the one lone window, it stood as a brave sign of life.

He worked his own land, bit by bit, as Thea helped to build a chicken coop, and fence to keep the few livestock that were their wedding gifts from friends. It was a helping community, and they knew they could count on their neighbors and on Thea's family. They lived the old adage, "One hand washes the other."

They were however, essentially alone. Out on the prairie, under the stars, the nearest farm three miles away, the work endless, they sang songs to keep up their spirits, said prayers together when they couldn't even make it to church on a Sunday, and grew together as only a farm couple could. Soon there was a baby to think of, and the good people of Stoneham to help every step of the way.

Memories of his younger days faded from Thomas' mind. He stopped thinking about Eva Jean within the year, and then couldn't remember her face. She was still an ache sometime. He knew he'd lost something special, but then he'd look at Thea and his son, and his heart felt calm. He was a lucky man. More so, because he knew it.

Eva Jean's world was different. She had always loved to learn and now, with so many scholars to think about and her own education her special joy, she worked as she had always done, putting everything into her learning and giving it back to her scholars in her teaching.

Dear Journal,

My work is my joy. I love my scholars every year and learn much from them. But it is as I study at Institute and Normal School that I have the greatest pleasure. I find that all those years of working with my hands making quilts and crochet have helped me learn better. I can sit for hours reading and studying just as I sit for hours with a needle in my hand. I get lost you might say, in books and quilts. When I get tired of plain old study, I still relax with a crochet or a square. I can remember real well too. Must be from learning all those directions when you crochet.

Now I'm learning about putting on plays. It's like putting a quilt together—making all the scenes come together in a whole, but each scene has to be just so—just like a quilt square has to be right or it won't all fit together. Only difference is—plays go—just disappear. Quilts are forever.

She made new friends all the time, and met many young men. But Eva Jean held fast to a dream, that someday she would meet the right person. Her values were strong. Even though times were changing and she was able to date young men at Institute or at Normal school, still it was a lonely life. But she counted her blessings and knew she was rich in friendship, laughter and learning.

Chapter Twenty Two

1915: Journal entry:

Aunt Stella wrote such a sweet letter. She asked, "Have you met your Prince yet?" But I have to answer, not yet. This fellow, Jimmy, keeps coming around and he is a charmer. I'm not sure how I feel about him though. He's a cheerful sort, always laughing. He is a real salesman. He says I'm real pretty without my glasses and I'm always taking them off when he's around. He believes that the country will depend more and more on selling stuff for houses like washers and vacuums and he's determined to be part of it. So he's off around the country selling all the time, but he says he comes to see me as soon as he can. He also says he puts money into the stock market to save for the future so he's always a little short on cash. I helped him out once, but I don't have much either, and what I have extra I send home.

We went to the show last week. It's only the second time I've seen a movie. It was called, The Birth of a Nation with the prettiest girl called Lillian Gish. Jimmy put his arm right around me in the movie which made me very nervous. I'm not sure he really understands that I can't let people think I have a special boyfriend. My job depends on it. I like him all right. It's not the same as it was with Thomas, but it could be. This is all so hard. My friend Laura gave our work up to go home and marry a neighbor recently widowed. He needed someone and wanted her. She feels he is her last chance. After all, she is 24. Maybe she is right, but I will miss her. I am 21. Is this my last chance?

The girls all noticed him as he fairly bounced up the steps of the school where the Institute for Teaching was held in Omaha. He wasn't handsome really; round-faced, a shock of sandy hair, but he seemed so confident, so happy that just looking at him made people smile. Yes, that was it. He had a happy face with a smile that would crack open any minute at a good joke or a pretty girl. At 5'4" he was just a bit taller than Eva Jean with eyes that seemed almost closed because he was always laughing.

Jimmy was a swell dresser. Yes indeed, he was always very neat, very tidy from his shoes to his straw boater. You didn't often see a man who was natty. You only read about them once in awhile in the paper. The few men going to the Institute were required to wear a shirt and tie, but the collars were mended and the ties and pants well worn. Jimmy definitely stood out and although he winked at a group of girls to his right as he bounced up the stairs and turned all the way round to admire a pretty girl on his left, he kept himself going right up those stairs. He knew exactly what he wanted. The pretty little teacher was sweet and smart, and just the right size. She earned a good living, and she looked very good on his arm once she let down her hair and took off those glasses. Besides, there was something about this little schoolmarm that was special. She was a real lady, and innocent besides. Jimmy found her irresistible.

There she was just coming out of her class, her students still holding her attention. He stopped and just looked at her. She was a petite girl, with a very slender, pretty shape. Jimmy noticed things like that.

"Hmm. I could fill her out a bit. She's almost too thin. And that dress! She'll look better in silk."

He smiled to himself remembering the snazzy silk nightgown he had bought with her in mind when he was in Kansas City.

"Wonder when I'll get her into it."

She saw him standing there, that little smile playing around his lips. She was so glad to see him that she smiled back, an open, happy smile that lit up her face and couldn't help but be noticed by the young girl at her side who turned to see who had so transformed her serious young teacher.

"Somebody's waiting for you Miss Carey. Looks like somebody special, I'd say."

That's all Eva Jean needed to return to her usual self.

"No, no, just a friend. Anything else you want to discuss about today's lecture, Grace?"

"Not a thing," the girl said. "You just have a real nice day now, Miss Carey." And she was off with a smile and giggle, down the hall.

"Aw shucks, Eva Jean that smile is all gone. Don't look so serious. Aren't you glad to see me?" Jimmy said as she approached him. His face was kind of scrunched up as he tried to pretend he was hurt.

He looked so funny trying to look sad, impossible for him to do, that she gave up and laughed again.

"OK fella'. You got me. Sure I'm glad to see you. When'd you get in? What are you doing here?"

"Got in this morning and came right over to see you. Why else would I be here?"

The next thing she knew he had whirled her into an empty classroom, closed the door grabbed her around the waist, removed her glasses and kissed her fast but hard behind the door which opened almost immediately crushing them behind it at which point Eva Jean dropped her papers.

He stepped out from behind the door and said to a bewildered student, "Be careful will ya'? Miss Carey here dropped her papers and we had to pick them up. Got 'em all Miss Carey?"

"Why!—why, no I don't."

She stood there completely befuddled, struggling to get her

glasses back on, while he commandeered two students to help him get the papers.

"Thank you," she said, unable to look at any one of them. "Thank you all very much." And she swept, with great dignity out the door.

As they continued to walk down the hall, Eva smiled cheerfully as people passed by, but said through clenched teeth.

"Are you crazy? I'll lose my job."

He just smiled at her. 'Aw gee, didn't you like it?"

"No I didn't like it. How do you think so fast anyhow?"

"You didn't like my kiss? Really?"

They were outside the building now and Eva her face still red, but now unsmiling answered as she turned to face him.

"I did like your kiss, very much thank you, but not in public."

"It wasn't in public Miss Schoolteacher. It was behind a door."

"James, you are impossible. The next time you come to town, for heaven's sake, let me know and I'll meet you somewhere. This is too much pressure."

"Fine, I will. Now let's get some lunch."

As always, Eva Jean had fun with him. He told the latest jokes, some of them just a bit off-color, but not so bad that she would be upset. He seemed to know how much she could tolerate. He minded his manners; no more rough sudden kisses, but he held her hand, and asked to see her the next day when she finished her class. She agreed. He stopped his car a block from her rooming house and asked very politely if he could kiss her. She was impressed. And she wanted a kiss. Oh, yes she did. The earlier one had been a surprise, but it was exciting too. There had been few kisses in her life, and his were special.

He leaned toward her, put his hand behind her neck and his finger stroked her cheek. He waited while he felt her breath on his cheek, while he felt the pulse in her neck begin to speed, then he moved his lips to hers and just brushed her lips. She gasped. She waited, and he moved to her again, but brushed against her cheek instead. He smelled so good, so different. What was that? It was the cleanest male scent she'd ever known. Jimmy wore shaving lotion. Bay Rum. It was new. It was a sign of a different class of man. Jimmy was very aware that it was for men who sought to be different. He also knew that women loved it. She caught her breath with a shudder. He felt it. Then he kissed her, and pulled her closer.

Her head reeled as she tasted his lips, felt his teeth, and his hand on her cheek, the other on her back pulling her closer.

"Oh, but this is wonderful," she barely thought. When he stopped, she leaned closer, the longing too great to put aside. Jim smiled to himself. And leaned in again. This time the kiss was long and searching, her lips parted, her heart pounding. She was lost in the moment, the feeling; the heat of his kiss. And he knew it. It wasn't easy, but he also knew he had to stop.

The next thing she knew she was at the rooming house, Jimmy saying good night, leading her carefully to the door when she could hardly stand, her knees felt so weak. Then she was in her own room and he was gone. Jimmy on the other hand found some friends, went out on the town to keep his own knees from shaking. He had a fine time and looked forward to the next day.

She was awake for hours remembering his kiss, smiling to herself, and shaking inside. The next day she was distracted and unfocused in class, looking forward to seeing him again.

It was Friday and she was free. She tried so hard not to let him know how she felt, but her heart raced just seeing him again. They drove off quietly toward the center of town where he had promised her dinner and a show; then home before it was late. All the women in college had curfews and she wouldn't dream of getting home later than 8:30 pm. She absolutely had to get home before the students whose curfew was at 9:00.

Dinner seemed to be rushed. Then he asked if she'd mind stopping at his place. Eva Jean assumed he meant that she'd wait outside for him, but he asked her to come in and see the room.

"No, no I couldn't Jim. Really no."

132

"Come on Teach, nobody's home. You already let your hair down. Don't be so skittish. I won't bite, but we'll have a chance for one great kiss. What d'ya say?"

He had that smile; that twinkle in his eye, the little dimple in the corner of his mouth and she just melted. She followed him into the house and into his room. The kiss was in fact just as delicious as it had been before, and the next thing you know, he was fumbling with her blouse, and she was weak-kneed again. But then, just as she pulled back and muttered a weak and barely heard "No." she saw the silk negligee spread out on the bed. And it all was clear.

She was still struggling to breathe when she said, "Oh, Jimmy you dope. I'm not as easy as all that."

She was out the door before he could stop her, but he tried. She was running then, out the door of the house, and down the street. Her heart was still pounding from the kiss, the sight of the nightgown, the suddenness of her understanding of his intentions. Tears blinded her as she ran and her emotions mixed with longing and anger. Why did he have to spoil it? As she came to the corner she had to stop running. How could she get back to her rooming house? She could lose her job. This was serious.

Suddenly, he was there beside her in the car.

"Get in Eva Jean."

"No, no, I can't trust you. No"

"You have to trust me, there isn't any other way to get you back. I'll be good I promise."

She stood on the corner feeling like a fool. She knew she had no choice. The next second she was sitting as far away from him as possible as he drove her back with all sorts of apologies and smiles and "You can't blame a guy for trying now, can you?"

As always, Jimmy was adorable.

Eva left him at the curb without answering and went straight to her room just minutes before the first student arrived home.

The next day after breakfast she was her old self. She had

been so exhausted, both from her sleepless night earlier, then the emotional turmoil of rejecting his advances that surprisingly, she had slept soundly and rose feeling refreshed and focused on her work.

She knew that he would be waiting for her after breakfast and she was right. But she didn't expect what he had to say.

"I have to go. I'm sorry I hurt you, but I can't stay around you like this. It's too hard. I'm not a teenager Eva Jean, I'm a man, and I can't play these games."

"So that's what it is to you? A game? It's my life you're playing your games with Jimmy. My life."

He looked at her for a long time. His smile was still there just at the corner of his lips.

"Sorry Sister, I must have been wrong about you. I thought you were a woman, not a little girl scared of herself, scared to love."

"Is that what this is? Love?" she asked.

As he looked into her earnest, open face, and those lovely eyes and heard the sincerity of her question; not asked in sarcasm which he could handle, but asked as a human being to him as the more expert, Jimmy instinctively felt wary.

"Careful here old Buddy," he told himself. "This is dangerous ground."

She could sense that he had no intention of answering her question.

"You may not think so, Jimmy, but I am a woman, and my reputation is all that keeps me working supporting my family and myself. I will not risk all that I am for you or for any man for that matter. Take care of yourself. And thanks for the good times. It was fun."

For a few seconds tears stung, but she walked resolutely away. She did not run. She walked toward the school where she knew she'd find some friends. She was back in the building surrounded by students before he could say another word.

Dear Journal,

> *Jimmy didn't love me. He just wanted to make love to me. I sent him away. It was a case of—Thank you. No thank you. Goodbye!*
> *Just as well. I can't really see without my glasses!! Now if only I can find some nice fellow who doesn't mind glasses, I'll be fine. A prince? Just a nice man will do. SIGH!*

Chapter Twenty Three

Letters: 1916

Dear Royal,

It's OK, dear brother. It really is OK for you and your sweetheart to have and love my quilt. It was made in such a happy time of my life with hope for the future and it should be used by you both for your own life ahead. It's sweet that you felt that I should keep it for my own "someday". Oh, I still have hope, but I will want something different.

Everything else in my old chest is gone now. But I have had a good time giving those special things to friends and it saved me buying many a wedding present! Even though I wear my hair in a bun now, and have to wear these terrible glasses, I haven't quite given up all hope yet. Don't you think that my handwriting is so much better now that I can SEE? I had no idea how poorly I was writing.

In fact, when I look back on the little journal you gave me so long ago, I realize that I have learned so much since then. I didn't realize that I spoke and wrote

so poorly. But I hope I'm better now and that I didn't
pass on too much of my own poor grammar to my scholars.
I am glad that you are planning your wedding soon.
You have worked so hard and are doing so well. I can't
wait to meet Katherine this summer in Pennsylvania
where I will study and you will be working. What a nice
thing to get to the East at last. Be well dear brother.

Fondly,
Eva Jeannette

LETTER, 1917

Dear Aunt Stella and Uncle Elroy,

I can't wait to see you both again. Royal and his
Katherine are so happy together in Pennsylvania that
it is a thrill to visit with them. They have such fun
together and they took me all through Philadelphia
and I saw the Liberty Bell! We are even going to take a
trip to Buffalo, New York where the whole city is
electrified and then to Niagara Falls to see the wonder
of the world! Imagine that! It is wonderful to be able
to travel and see my country. It will help me in my
teaching.

You ask if I am lonely. Yes, I am lonely sometimes,
and I do long for a home of my own. I have met many
young men through my studies, but often they are
"kooks" or mashers. That is the new slang, which I
have learned on my travels. I do have an assured feeling
that someday the things that I long for will be mine.
Lack of them have developed a patience which I most
certainly did not possess. I'm not unhappy or blue as I
was a few years ago. No one can take away from me,
the appreciation of LIFE which has grown with me. I

can always make my own living, one better than the average, and I feel competent that one day I will be a homemaker. I can't help wondering. What will the New Year bring? Here is my latest fancy learnin' for you, Au revoir!

You niece, the book worm.
Eva Jean

LETTER 1918

Our Dear Girl,

Not so good at letter writin. Me and Elroy want you to know that we have great faith in you. You will find the right fella someday. He's out there and you just have to be ready when he comes.

We're so proud of you, Eva Jean, getting a real education. Don't know how you managed to learn so much at normal school and do your teaching too. But you done it. Your Mama would be so proud.

Rains' good. The larks is singing. Looks to be a good season. Elroy and me can't wait to see our gal. Come home soon.

Stella and Elroy

Chapter Twenty Four

Wonderful to visit Royal and Katherine again. They have built a whole bedroom around my quilt. I am so pleased. My hand-work isn't going so well these days, as I work too hard to get my degree and to prepare for my students, and to direct my plays, which raise money for charity. It all works well, but there isn't much time to do needlework anymore. My hope chest languishes at home.

Home. My home is still Elm Creek. I'm often far away depending on where I am teaching which so far has taken me all over Nebraska and even to Pennsylvania. But I couldn't wait to get back to the sounds of the people of my own country—Nebraska—my people, my home.

Now I am to start to teach an adult class at Institute. It is good that I have the experience of directing plays because it showed them that I could work with adults as well as children. We'll just wait and see what this new experience brings.

She was just a bit nervous, but as always with Eva Jean, she was eager to teach and to make new friends of her scholars. She was at the front of the room, all her adult students before her, calling out their names when he came in. She looked up to see him and almost caught her breath. "My now, there's a good—looking fellow," she thought.

She gestured for him to take a seat, started the class and it rolled along with her lecture, the readings, the list of books to be covered, and some exercises for them to work at before the next class. With all her experience with plays, she had become a wonderful reader. She could make a text come to life with her phrasing, her easy dialects when needed, and the quality of her voice, which was pleasantly feminine, but not high pitched. In truth, when Miss Carey read, her listeners were mesmerized.

The class ended on a note of cheerful laughter, and she turned to the task of organizing her papers and looked up finally to see him standing there, quietly, a smile on his face. Was she aware that she automatically reached up to take off her glasses as she said?—

"Why yes, Mr. Whitmer isn't it? How can I help you?"

"Miss Carey, you read wonderfully well. Made it all come to life."

"Well now, how kind. Thank you very much." He stood there not saying anything while she looked up at him, waiting.

"I—ah—I understand that you direct plays. Will you be doing one before the summer's over? I like amateur theatrics myself, and I'd like to know if there might be a part in it for me. I thought I'd try out."

"Well, certainly. I'm not sure just what we're going to do, but I'll announce it soon."

She couldn't know that he had never acted before in his life, nor, until that minute, had he even considered doing such a thing. Of course he didn't know that until he asked, she had had no intentions of doing a play that summer either.

The Journal

Well now. Something happened today. A man came into my class of literature. He is one of those older students who come from time to time. His name is Willard, but they call him Will.

He is very sweet, I think. He was in the war but he was shot in the shoulder and couldn't go back. He wants to be a teacher too, but he is an artist. I found all this out by asking some questions of others. He has the nicest eyes, and the nicest voice too, and we all think that he is very good looking. Well now, that is nice of course. I'm going to do a play after all. I think it will be another melo-drama. I think this handsome fellow will be in it. I think my life is turning upside down. What little journal, almost—running—out—of—pages, do you think of that?

Chapter Twenty Five

1920

The day was glorious, the sun incredibly warm on her skin; the fields on both sides of the road full of the flowers that came like a blessing after the long winter.

Royal had picked her up at the train station as usual in a brand new car belonging to Uncle Elroy.

As usual, she'd thrown herself into her brother's arms and he'd lifted her up like she was a little doll. When she was with Royal she was never a dignified lady teacher, she was just a kid again with the brother she loved.

Royal was taller now. He'd shot up late as many boys do, and reached his full height at 21. Eva Jean was always surprised now when she saw him. She was still so small, so light.

They caught up in minutes, as he whisked her luggage up and directed her into the car. They almost babbled their news

"Katherine's at the house. We had a great train trip. Stopped along the way, and I took pictures too. I'm learning to develop them myself. I can take pictures of all of us, isn't that great?"

"Pictures! That's wonderful, Will will be here later and I can't wait for you two to meet. I know you're going to love him."

Their constant letters kept them up to date for the most part. He knew all about Will—how he'd survived the front lines by getting shot and sent home. He knew what a good artist he was, and how he'd sold many of his paintings in Chicago where he'd been living since the war. Like most young men who didn't get called, Royal couldn't wait to hear about his experiences "over there." But Eva Jean had warned him that he didn't like to talk about it so Royal wouldn't press. He knew that the war had changed this 25 year old, and that he'd decided against a career in the fast growing new business of advertising. Will also had had enough of living in a big city. Now he wanted a simpler country life, hopefully teaching art in a college with time to make a home and family and do his own painting.

Eva Jean turned her face to the sun and smiled up into it. Her hair was free again. It curled around her face and blew in the wind lifting and swirling around her shoulders. It had darkened some over the years, but every spring it became streaked with the sun and it seemed to shimmer in the sunlight. Will loved her hair. He loved how it framed her lovely eyes, how it felt in his hands.

Eva Jean thought of that—how he'd hold her hair as he kissed her. The whole year flashed by in her mind as she and Royal bumped along the road. She remembered the day they met and the play that followed. Will had designed a simple set when it became clear that he was definitely not an actor. They had worked together, laughed together, and fell in love together day by day in front of all their friends who were happy for them both.

She touched the ring on her hand, the antique amethyst surrounded with pearls and set on a wide band engraved in ivy.

"Ivy means forever, Eva Jean. Like you and me will be, forever. It's not modern. I hope that's OK. Do you like it?"

Did she like it? It took her breath away.

"It's perfect. You picked it just for me, and it's perfect. I love it."

Royal glanced down at it as they drove. He saw her gaze at it with a quiet joy and recognized the contentment in her smile. He didn't say anything; just reached over and patted her hand. They grasped hands for a minute or two and just grinned, brother and sister understanding one another without a word.

They pulled up to the house and Eva Jean jumped out of the car like a young girl, and although she started to help Royal with the bags he just said,

"Oh, go on—I'll bring them. Go!"

She ran up the long front path and was met at the door by a beaming Aunt Stella.

"Well, our darling girl. Made it home at last! Come in come in."

And she stepped into the door and into

Surprise! Surprise!

Instead of just the family, the house was bulging with everyone she knew. They all crowded around her everyone talking at once. Why, there was Katherine of course, and her sisters, Leona and Viola. Here was Mrs. Kenny who nursed her through her illness, and Anna, all grown and a teacher herself now. There were the mothers of all of her first little scholars,—the kiddies, she had called them. Mrs. Anderson gave her such a hug. Was that Joseph in the background? Of course it was. And Sarah, absolutely lovely girl at 18 soon would be his bride. Even Mrs. Arnott was there. There was Will's Mother, Mary Whitmer, and his sister Edythe. Altogether there were 26 women, and with Uncle Elroy, Royal and Joseph there were 30 people crowded into the small front parlor, spilling over into the dining room.

"Where's the groom? Where's Will?"

"Oh, he'll be here." Mrs. Whitmer said. "He planned on giving us time for just the girls, first. I think he's a little overwhelmed."

"Oh, Eva Jean, we're all so glad you came home to be married. We can't wait for your big day. We'll all be there."

The party was all her dreams come true. Eva Jean just glowed in her pretty pink dress, that she had made special for her trousseau with the delicate lace collar and cuffs. With it, she wore tiny pearls in her ears that matched her ring. She had a tiny bit of lip rouge on, but the blush in her cheeks was all her own. She looked lovelier than she had on that day long ago, when she was 18.

Sitting in the corner was her hope chest. Uncle Elroy had polished it till it glowed and her gifts were piled all around it.

"Time to fill this thing up again, girl" Elroy said. "Didn't spend all that time on it to have it go empty."

What wonderful gifts they were! One after the other, she opened such lovely things. A full set of glassware, candlewick design in three different shapes, and linens for their bed. Beautiful silk blouses for her trousseau, and towels like the ones she had given away. Many things were hand made. Finally, Mrs. Arnott handed her a special gift.

"I hope you can accept this Eva Jean. Willa Mae sent it. She wants you to have it. She says—well, you'll see."

Eva Jean hardly knew what to say. She opened the gift slowly, and found in it a square picture frame of gold gilt. In it was a padded background in pink silk with a beautiful handkerchief deftly sewn to show it's lovely double crocheted border.

The note said.

Dear Eva Jean,

I kept it. You made it for me. Do you remember? I thought that you should have it now. These picture frames are the latest thing to show off really fine workmanship. I hope that you will accept it from me, with my fond remembrance of a friendship from long ago. I enclose a picture of my Mr. Hancock, and our three little ones.

Yours, Willa Mae.

The picture was of an older man with a long mustache, and three very fat little children. In the midst was a still smiling, still dimpled, still dark-haired Willa Mae. But Willa Mae was no longer plump and delicate. She was very round indeed. In fact, Willa

146

Mae was huge! Her delicate little face was lost in rolls of chin and cheeks.

Mrs. Arnott said. "She has a little weight problem now, but that's because of three children in four years. She's real happy in Denver. Her husband's a minister, very prominent there. We worked on mounting the hanky together Eva Jean. I hope you'll like it."

Eva Jean was astounded. Not only because of the picture of her friend, but because she hadn't thought of Willa Mae in a very long time. She had forgiven her long ago. It didn't matter any more.

"It's a lovely gift Mrs. Arnott. Thank you both so much" and she got up and gave Mrs. Arnott a kiss and whispered in her ear. "Thank you for coming. Say hello to Willa Mae for me. It's all right now. It all worked out for the best. Tell her I said so, will you?"

"Thank you my dear. I always said you were a fine girl, Eva Jean. Always said so. I think that Willa Mae got a little tired of hearing me say so, in fact." And she patted her hand.

"We'll eat just as soon as your Will comes Eva Jean. Come see how pretty the table looks." Stella said as they passed into the dining room to view the table, laden with wonderful things.

There was a ham, cured at the smokehouse of the farm next to theirs, juicy and pink with cloves marking diamonds of fat. There was a huge tray of Aunt Stella's lighter than air biscuits, and large dish of candied yams. Stella had thought twice about the candied yams. "Too sweet." She'd thought, but Elroy prevailed. They were one of his favorites. Green beans were just beginning to come in, so there was a bean salad with green and yellow beans and slivers of onion with mustard and vinegar dressing. It seemed like every woman there had contributed a dessert. The side-board held them all. There were fruit pies, strawberry and rhubarb, an apple crumb and a peach made from last year's put up peaches. There were trays of cookies, and wonderful cakes, chocolate and even spice with a brown sugar frosting. It all looked wonderful. Eva Jean had never seen such a feast in her Aunt's house and she went to her and kissed her and put her arms around her and just held her.

"How can I ever thank you Auntie?" This is a feast for a queen."

"Well now, nobody ever treated you even like a princess, girl, but this is one time we can pretend. It does look pretty good doesn't it?"

There was one more treat in store for the bride-to-be.

Since the house was all taken up with people, Aunt Stella had put the quilting frame out on the back porch. One by one, she'd asked people to go out and embroider their names on a special quilt. All afternoon, everyone worked for a few minutes each, stitching their names on a quilt top that Stella had put together over the last year. The quilting would come later, and when it was finished it would hold the names of everyone present that day. Even Royal had put his name on it, and Joseph put on his initials, and Uncle Elroy, designed a little star with Elroy, next to it. Now they all led her out to see it at last.

It was a fine quilt, done in the log cabin pattern, worked in materials that Stella had found left over from many of Eva Jean's own sewing projects combined with fabrics that she had chosen from the bolts in Arnott's General Store.

Eva Jean had tears in her eyes when she saw it, and realized that around it's perimeter were the names of all of her special friends. She kissed each person there, thanking them over and over.

She heard the horn just then. And she couldn't wait to see him. "There he is—Oh, excuse me—there he is!"

And she almost ran to the front door. The guests all followed her to the front parlor and gathered near the windows as she ran down the walk.

"Oh my!" Mrs. Arnott, said.

"Well, she sure did get a right pretty one, I'll say that" sister Viola offered.

Unfolding his long legs from the car was just about the best-looking fellow these folks had ever seen. Tall and lanky, you could call him, with dark wavy hair that fell over his brow, and a broad smile that crinkled his eyes as he looked down at this tiny girl. He took her hand and folded her arm in his as they started their walk toward the house.

She was beaming, and she took his arm and they could see that she was chattering away at him, laughing and happy. He couldn't take his eyes off her. Then he stopped for a minute and looked all around the place. They couldn't hear him, but it was clear he was admiring the land around. He gestured up to the sky.

"Why Eva Jean look at the light. It's just beautiful. Oh, I'd like to paint this. It's sort of pink isn't it? What a great place."

"Eva Jean's eyes filled up with tears."

"What is it? I'm not making you sad am I?" and he cupped her face in his hands. In the window more than one woman caught her breath at the gentleness of the gesture.

"Oh, no,—No!" she said, wiping a tear away.

"I'm just so happy to have you here—and to have you see the light like this."

He wiped the tear from her eye with his finger. She knew all along she'd see that light again someday, but she'd never dreamt that he could see it too.

"Come on—Come on in. They're all waiting to meet you."

Chapter Twenty Six

New York 1995

"I was named after her!" Jeannie was stunned. Her name was spelled the same. Dad must have insisted on carrying over the name. She was officially Jeannette, but everyone had called her Jeannie since she was just a girl. She was proud to bear the name of this prairie teacher, this wonderful, brave, loyal woman who had met the man of her dreams in a classroom more than half a century ago.

Dear Cousin Sally,

I wonder if you can tell me any more about Aunt Eva. The journal is fantastic. It's the most wonderful gift I've had in such a long time. It's so fragile, but I'm very careful with it. I have it wrapped in some non-acid paper now so it doesn't disintegrate any more. Some of the writing is really hard to read, but I'm carefully transcribing it every chance I get. Have you read it? I can't believe all she went through so long ago, or how difficult everything was then. It seems so impossible that she could have lost her lover because of a storm. Isn't that incredible? But now I've just got to know more about her and Will Whitmer. Were they really happy together? I know you are far too busy, but I'd be so grateful if you could send me any information you have.

Thanks Sally, Go out and look at those stars for me will you?

Love, Jeannie

PS Did you know that I am Jeannette too? I must have been named for her. I only just realized that.

Dear Cousin Jeannie,

Sure, we all knew you were named after Eva Jean. Why do you think we wanted you to have the journals? We thought, since you took the time to come here never even knowing us, that you would be interested and caring enough to take good care of them. We all think they are special even though I don't know who has read them in many years.

Eva Jean was always a teacher though she went from teaching on the prairie to teaching in the institutes to teaching at college here at the University in Omaha.

She also was well known for her directing in Little Theatre throughout the West She traveled all over directing plays when she wasn't teaching and established a theatre department here at the University.

Will taught too. He was a fine artist. His work still hangs in the library there. He was popular at one time and his stuff sold well here in the West. But he too made his real living as a teacher. They traveled a lot but always came back to the prairie. It was in her blood, I think. She couldn't stay away too long. Her brother Royal, your Grandfather, was the only one who left and never returned. All us cousins are still around here living in Nebraska or Colorado.

They didn't have children, but Aunt Eva always said we were all her children and she was awfully good to everyone, particularly her family's kids. She helped send many of us to college. They were married for 60 years, and we always remember them so sweet to one another. Will would take flowers to her and put them on her pillow, and she would leave him little love notes. Theirs was a real love story.

Jeannie, I just might take you up on your offer to visit. Jimmy can't leave the farm, but my Mom and Dad will take the kids this summer for a whole week, and I'd like a chance to get away. What do you think? It would just be for a few days. I know I can't leave here for very long. I'd miss the stars too much!

You do see SOME stars in New York City don't you?

Love, Sal

To *fishers@libsearch.com*: Many thanks for info. Do you know what happened to friendship quilt? Of course you can come. June maybe? Take care.

To *careyj@bluepoint.com:* Got me going re the quilt. I've no idea. Will start a search for it. Where could it be?

To *careyj@bluepoint.com:* I found it! It was in bottom of old wooden chest she gave me years ago. I had it all along stored in barn. No idea quilt was there. It's beautiful. Just so lovely, faded but still fine. Glad you asked. Do you want it? Is first week in June OK?

Jeannie received this last message at her desk. She closed her door then, and sat by herself just remembering so many details from her visit in April. She saw Sally and the house she lived in and suddenly she remembered so many things she saw there that she hadn't asked about. It was a fine old farmhouse, updated of course, with a wonderfully appointed kitchen that would be just a dream for anyone living in an apartment in New York City.

There was still the well out in the back and wonderful old trees surrounding the house in the middle of prairie land. Sally's life seemed to be filled with old things. She was surrounded with antiques. Her own mother's ice-box, all refinished gleamed with its brass fittings. Jeannie had slept in a brass bed that Sally had restored under other, hand-made quilts.

For the first time Jeannie felt a twinge of envy for her cousin. Sally had everything that Jeannie longed for; a family, children, work that satisfied her. She smiled often and Jeannie had noticed the kisses between her and Virgil exchanged furtively in the farmhouse kitchen. It was Sally who was the real inheritor of Eva Jean's courage, her creativity, her determination. Jeannie felt like the lost sheep. But she had a tremendous desire to know her cousin better.

To *fishers@libsearch.com:* **re quilt. NO. It belongs to you without question. Enjoy. The old wooden chest. Is it her hope chest do you think? And June—first week is fine.**

Chapter Twenty Seven

Reclamation

After Omaha, things had changed for Jeannie. She could breathe again. The pain, the inability to think was gone. She forgot all about seeing a therapist and she could sleep again. Eva Jean was alive to her. She saw her, or thought she did, as a young girl, then a young woman who had suffered terrible loss and had survived to love again. Jeannie copied Eva Jean's letter to Aunt Stella and hung it next to her computer where she didn't even have to pull it up to see it.

> *"I do have an assured feeling that someday the things that I long for will be mine. Lack of them have developed a patience which I most certainly did not possess. No one can take away from me, the appreciation of LIFE which has grown within me."*

It became her mantra. And suddenly Jeannie was seeing her world in a new way. She stopped going to the gym every evening at 7:00 and instead took a real lunch hour and went out to walk every day. She looked at everything around her—people, buildings and she began to see things in New York City that she had been blind to before.

She began to discover, "up." There is of course, the NYC that most New Yorkers see everyday. You don't look higher than their shoulder. You look at people in passing so you don't bump into them, but you don't look at them to actually see them. You see store windows, street corners and DON'T WALK signs. The world knows however, that only a New Yorker does indeed cross the street when the light says not to. Most of all, you rush—going very fast from block to block, cab to place, or subway to stairs, to street to elevator, to halls to offices or apartments. But you don't look up—not if you live there. You don't look up—ever.

Unless you are a tourist.

Jeannie was becoming a tourist in her own city. She was learning the difference between Beaux Arts architecture, (Grand Central Station) and Ars Nouveau, (Rockefeller Center) and American Victorian, the mansions of 5th Avenue, uptown.

She signed up for walking tours on the weekends and was learning things about how the city was built that she'd had no clue about.

In one week she walked Central Park around the reservoir and lunched with her friend Julie at the World Trade Center. Julie had just started there and she wore a white patch behind her ear to settle her stomach, she said.

"It sways."

"Huh?"

"The building, it sways in the wind. They say I'll get used to it, but I'm wearing a dramamine patch for awhile."

"How do you know, maybe it's your imagination?"

"No." Julie explained. "The pictures on the wall. They move. Really."

Jeannie was seeing everything as if she had only just moved there. She was falling in love with New York all over again.

She was beginning to meet a whole new group of people, not all young and striving in business as she had always been, but interesting people nevertheless.

One of them was a woman who ran a program for mentoring girls from disadvantaged families, who were struggling to stay in school. Carole was petite, blonde and blue eyed; a no-nonsense kind of woman, but fun too. Not-for-profits didn't pay great salaries, but Carole loved her work. She went on the local trips to learn more about day trips that would be appropriate for her mentors and girls. She took a lot of notes, and after the second trip together she asked Jeannie if she might be interested in mentoring or perhaps interest some people from her office. Jeannie wasn't very comfortable about getting involved with alienated girls. "I wouldn't know how to even talk to them but I'll talk to my boss about it and see if she'll let me give out some info."

She had started to ask around about the publishing business. Did anybody know any one in the business? Who could she talk to about a book based on the journals? But she didn't have a clue where to start and wasn't getting very far. And she found that she missed Sally. They were writing whenever they could, and e-mailing which was easier. Now she had the confidence that she could show her a good time, so she was truly thrilled to see her cousin come through the door at the LaGuardia gate. This time they hugged like long lost sisters.

They sat up late catching up on the farm, Jeannie's job, and talked—it seemed like forever—about Eva Jean. Jeannie read aloud from the letters and they carefully unfolded the handkerchief. It wasn't in a frame and had just a speck of antique rust on it. The double row of fine crochet was on it so they decided it must have been the one she'd made for Willa Mae. They couldn't be sure but they both hoped it was.

On Saturday morning they hurried downtown on the subway to Battery Park to pick up a boat on a special tour up the Hudson to Sunnyside, the home of Washington Irving. Since Sally loved books, Jeannie had thought that she would enjoy seeing the tiny Dutch house that was an early American writer's home. It was a great way to see Manhattan from the water's edge too. Sally just loved the place. She'd had no idea there was such a tranquil spot so close to the big city.

Some of the people she'd met before were on the trip and they had easy conversations with a couple of them. Her new friend Carole introduced them to somebody new. His name was Sam. He was divorced with two kids who lived with their mother, and on weekends when he didn't have the girls, he often took these day trips usually with a friend. This day he was alone. He was in publishing.

"Ask him!" Carole said.

"But I don't even know the man." Jeannie said. "This is recreation, I can't get into business stuff with him."

"Sure you can. Ask him."

Jeannie looked at Sally, took a breath and plowed right in.

"Ah, I suppose I shouldn't ask this, but since you're in publishing—Do you know any writers who might be interested in developing a story based on old journals ?"

"I beg your pardon?"

"Oh, I'm sorry, but I just wondered. There probably isn't even a market for this stuff. It's historical though—a real piece of American history. We, that is, my cousin and I, want to find a way to get our Aunt's journals published and we haven't a clue how to go about it." She felt like a perfect tourist, which in New York speak meant a total clod.

She added, "But this isn't a good time. Sorry to bother you."

He smiled, a bit forced Jeannie thought.

"I'm sorry, but you're right this isn't a good time. Let's just do the tour first and when we have lunch we can talk about it OK?" He smiled more pleasantly, then got up and walked away.

Sally turned to her and said. "Well, to quote Eva Jean. 'That went well, don't you think?'" They both started to laugh and couldn't stop.

At lunch they had forgotten about it, and sat down together back on the boat for a boxed lunch, when Sam came by.

"Hi. I said, I'd talk about your book, but first things first. Who are you?"

Sally explained as best she could about their grand aunt and he listened patiently.

"Tell you what. I've got people in my office who do the reading. When you think you've got it in some kind of readable condition, call me and I'll promise that you get a reading of it. I can't offer anything else." He handed them his card.

They thanked him. He left. That was it.

"I guess there's a lot of work to do on it before it's in any kind of 'readable condition.' Don't you think, Sally"?

"Maybe now you know why we thought you were the one to have them, Jeannie. Most of us don't even have computers yet. Good Luck Cuz!"

"Oh thanks a lot." But Jeannie knew she wasn't going to let it go. Somehow she'd find a way to get them into some kind of readable status. Now if she could just find some time.

Sally's week whizzed by. She loved the Metropolitan Museum where Jeannie sent her one day. And she soon learned how to negotiate uptown and downtown. Sometimes she came out of the subway not sure which was north or south but that was only because the buildings cut out the sun and she couldn't know by instinct which direction she was in as she did on the prairie. Phantom of the Opera, was her first Broadway play and took her into a world she had only dreamed about, but she actually yelled aloud when the chandelier came crashing down to the stage, just as the director had planned.

She couldn't get over the size of Jeannie's apartment. It was tiny, or so she thought. Actually to a New Yorker it wasn't bad. It was long and actually had two bedrooms in it. She also didn't quite believe that the two little cabinets and a sink were really a kitchen.

"This is the kitchen?" Jeannie nodded.

"It's neat! I guess." She sounded so tentative that Jeannie could only laugh.

"Do you cook?" Sally asked.

"Well, that's a secret of New York City. The kitchens are so tiny no one can possibly keep enough food to eat, so everyone has to eat out all the time, which is wonderful for the economy. Then, of course, our places are so small no one actually wants to come home so we all work hideously long hours making the economy even better." She said it so seriously that for a minute

Sally believed her. Then she cracked up, and the two of them laughed together.

"OK, OK, so I'm a hick from Nebraska, but my gosh, your world is different Jeannie." They went out to dinner every night. Uptown to B. Smith's, downtown to the bistro's at the Chelsea Market. Sally savored every day. There was only one thing wrong.

"Sally, you look so tired. Can't you sleep?" Jeannie asked.

"Nuts. You weren't supposed to figure that out." Sally said. Everything is so close here. And when we go out the buildings loom like giants over everything. I guess I just feel claustrophobic. "Gimme land lot's a land," she started to sing.

By Wednesday, she was more than ready to go home although she had loved getting to know her cousin, seeing New York City and really hearing the journals read aloud for the first time. They had pieced some of it together and tried to make sense of some of the gaps figuring out where Eva Jean was when she wrote it. They hadn't even read some of the letters in the bottom of the box. It would take a while to rewrite it all and figure out the hand writing in a lot of places.

They stood together in the airport locked in a hug that wouldn't quit. Jeannie would miss her.

"Jeannie, now that we've read her diary, I have to tell you that I think that the wooden box in the barn is in fact the hope chest."

Jeannie was thrilled. "Really! That's so exciting. Is it OK? I mean, is it still in one piece?"

"Oh, yeah," Sally replied. "But it definitely needs work. The top is split from things being piled on it for all these years. Virgil can replace the top of it when he has a chance and can order the wood. It's got to be cherry and we don't have any of that on the farm. It is a fine piece in spite of the wear, and I think we can restore it beautifully. Jeannie, will you take it when it's done? She gave it to me, but Aunt Eva always said that gifts were meant to be shared. She loved giving things away, that's something I learned from her. I think it will just fit under your window in the apartment. I'd like you to have it. I'm sure Aunt Eva would like that too."

159

Jeannie was so moved she couldn't speak.

"I—I" was all she could muster as they held onto one another till the last minute that Sally had before she boarded.

On the way back to the apartment Jeannie felt lonely. She was really going to miss her friend and cousin. But she felt that she had Eva Jean for company in a strange way. Every time she re-read parts of the journal more and more came alive.

Her real work was going along fine now that she was on top of her game again. But it was no longer exciting work for her. She simply no longer cared if she made it to the top of the advertising business any more. The power lunches were fine, but suddenly it was all a case of "been there-done that." She wanted, and now knew she needed, a change. How to do it?

For a time she just continued as she had been, cutting back on her work hours, hoping no one would notice, and spending time at the computer with the journals.

Mostly though, she was spending more and more time out and about New York City. She didn't want to frequent the bars she usually went to. Had no desire to eat out with her old friends when she discovered that they had absolutely no interest in the journals what so ever. None. She had bored them to death with talk of it.

She signed up for writing courses at the Gotham School and was having a great time writing up a storm; not only the journals but stories of her own too. She sent them all to Sally who critiqued them and sent them back. It was fun. She loved it. With the people from her class, Carole, and some of the people she had met on the tours, she had a small, but new group of friends.

Chapter Twenty Eight

Beginnings

She hadn't thought of him at all for a good two months when the letter arrived literally begging her to see him again and accept his apology. With the letter was notification that investments he had made for her months earlier had split, and she was making a good profit. It was just like Brad. Charming, witty, properly contrite. He was quite a salesman.

Jeannie sat down to write him a note. She thought about it for just a few seconds and then wrote it out with a smile on her face. It said:

> **Dear Brad,**
> **Thanks,**
> **No Thanks,**
> **Goodbye.**
> **Jeannie.**

She was very proud of herself.

"Thanks Aunt Eva Jean."

Jeannie needed the money. With it she could make some new plans for herself. She was going to go back to school and take more classes in writing. Her degree was in Communications, the famous, "And what will you do with it?" major, but it was because she was such a good writer that her advertising work went so well.

She felt more comfortable than she ever had before. Within a few months, she had a great start on filling in the gaps in Eva Jean's journals. She felt good about it so far, but she knew she needed help.

It was a glorious Fall day when she joined the tour group again with Carole for a trip way uptown—way, way uptown to a fabulous old estate called Wave Hill. It was one of the earliest fine homes on the Hudson, and on a day that held the sun, shimmering golden on gardens that still bloomed roses she saw the publisher again. "Sam,—Yes, Sam," she thought. That was his name. His girls were with him too. "Cute kids," she thought. "Must be about 6 and 8 or so."

They broke the busload of people into smaller groups for several private tours of the house and grounds, and there they were, right in her group. She smiled at him tentatively, sure that he wouldn't know her. But surprisingly he smiled back at her and when they started the walk through he said, "I thought I'd see you sooner. You were going to bring in a book. It was some kind of diary wasn't it? What happened?"

"I'm surprised you remembered."

"I remembered you. Jeannie isn't it?"

"Yeah, that's me. The book, well—it's still not ready. I'm the one who has to get it in some kind of shape as a real story. I work full time, and I've started some courses to get the skills to do it. There isn't much time to work on it. In fact, I should be home now working on it, but—" she looked around. "I'm glad I'm not. The day is glorious isn't it?" she asked.

"It certainly is."

I need some help, I think. I'm not really professional enough to do this. But I'm determined to try."

"Dad, can't we go outside. I don't wanna see a house."

He looked at Jeannie and shrugged. "This is Dana, and this is Kaitlin," he said.

The girls smiled shyly.

"Come on Dad, let's go outside."

"OK, we will. You go on ahead."

"Have fun girls," Jeannie said.

"Why don't you bring in what you've got."

"I'd really appreciate your help."

"Well, I don't know what I can do, but let's take a look at it. Oh, here's my card," and he handed it to her again as the group leader looked back to see where they were and his daughter called "Daa—ad"

Carole was watching the two of them.

"Very nice guy don't you think?" She asked. Jeannie nodded. She looked back at him as he left and said,

"Good looking guy too, don't you think?"

About 34 or so, she thought. Just about 6 feet. He had a fine, gentle smile, and gorgeous eyes. They were light brown, like butterscotch and he looked directly at her.

You could tell a lot about a guy the way he looked at you. Brad had had a habit of not looking at her. He would look away or over her shoulder or her head and not at her. She kidded him about it. "Hey, big guy", she'd say. "I'm here." He'd laugh and look at her then, but never for long. He didn't want to miss anything he'd always said. When she had found out he had cheated on her, she knew what it was that he didn't want to miss.

There wasn't really time to talk to Sam again, but Jeannie watched him with the girls as the day went by and realized that he was a very appealing man. He was easy and funny with them, holding hands, and letting them pretty much do what they wanted. At one point Jeannie quietly left the group. She just wanted to be outdoors so she took a short walk in one of the gardens just as he came around the corner with the girls.

"I guess this wasn't such a great idea to take little girls to a fancy mansion, but they love it out here."

The girls ran off again.

"I was kind of hoping I'd see you again. Maybe we could

have dinner together or something. Talk about the book, what do you think?"

Jeannies' heart did a little blip. He was looking at her kind of hesitantly, waiting for her answer.

"Dinner." She cleared her throat. "Why yes, that would be nice."

"May I have your number? I'll call."

She fumbled in her bag, ended up writing her number on a scrap of paper, saw his face relax and a real smile appear. He was pleased.

"Hmmm." Jeannie thought. "This is very nice."

Carole appeared just as the group tour was ending.

On the way home the little one fell asleep at his side, and he and the bigger girl, what was her name again—Kaitlin, chatted comfortably.

Carole told her how well two people were working out as mentors from Jeannie's office. "You sure you wouldn't like to take on a girl? You have an awful lot to give." She'd asked again.

It was late that night when she called Carole.

"About the mentoring thing, I think you're right. I would like to meet a girl and get to know her. If she likes me, maybe it would be something I could do for somebody for a change instead of just thinking about myself. I don't have much time right now, but I will have."

"You're going back to school aren't you?" Lisa asked.

"Yeah—the New School, I think. I don't need a Master's or anything. I just want to get more writing skills. There's no reason why I have to stay at this job forever. I can afford to take some time off, go to school and then look for something else, and who knows, maybe I can actually get published if I have the time to work at it."

"Tell you what. Since you've actually said yes, I don't want to lose you. I'll put your name on my list for the New Year, and in January we'll set something up. In the meantime you can get yourself re-organized."

"That's great. Just great. Thanks."

It was late as she hung up the phone and sat down at the computer to send a long letter to Sally to tell her what she'd decided. She had just finished when she looked up at the quote she'd taken out of the diary and hung just above the screen.

"I do have an assured feeling that someday the things that I long for will be mine. Lack of them have developed a patience which I most certainly did not possess. No one can take away from me, the appreciation of LIFE which has grown within me."

"Well Eva Jean, I'm feeling a lot more assured too, thanks to you. And I think that even I can be patient now. Something's going to happen, I know it. And as you would say, "no one can take away from me, the appreciation for the opportunity that lies ahead." Thanks old girl."

The face that reflected back at her in the darkened computer screen was almost like seeing Eva Jean herself, with her thick wavy hair, and her twinkling eyes.

Three hours away in Omaha, Sally and Virgil were just finishing dinner. It was twilight and stars just coming out. "You know honey, I keep thinking about Jeannie. She's been through a lot, but she seems to want some real change in her life. You know, she's so sharp and sophisticated, but I know that she really likes us. And I think Aunt Eva Jean's journals have been something very special to her."

"Do you really think that she'll have time to do something with them?" Virgil asked.

"She already has."

He reached over and put his hand on her shoulder as she put down the last dish, and they stood looking out the window at the first stars.

"Star light," Sally said.

"Star bright," Virgil added.

"I wish I may, I wish I might, have the wish, I wish tonight." Sally finished.

"And what is that, prairie woman?"

"Can't tell. Won't come true."

"Bet it's got something to do with your cousin."

She nodded.

"You want her to come out here. Right?"

She nodded again.

He looked at her and smiled as he thought deeply, "And I'll bet you, you want her to come with somebody special."

She smacked him playfully on the shoulder. "Oh, you. Do you have to read me that well? A girl can't have any secrets around a guy like you. What are you, clairvoyant?"

He nibbled on her ear as they turned to go out the door. "Nope. Just know you. You like to share the good stuff,"

"Oh, and you're the good stuff are you?"

"You got that right, but she's got to get her own." and they laughed together as they went outside.

Epilogue

Will's Letter

My Dearest Eva Jean,

Sitting in a fox-hole, with terrible noise all around, I didn't think that I would ever know happiness again. I was even glad to get shot and get out of there. But you make me smile just thinking of you. I love the way your hair curls all around your face. The way your eyes get all sparkly when you laugh. When you read and you focus so hard you don't even hear me, I just love that too.

Eva Jean, we have both come a long way. We both know what is really important.

Now don't you worry about letting Stella and Elroy down if you decide to stop working some day. I'll always be willing to help them out. My paintings are selling already. There is a market for my scenes or our country and its people. Soon, I too can teach. We'll be all right.

I'm glad you weren't scared to see my shoulder. It's not pretty, I know, but at least it's my left and if it gets bad someday I can still paint. As long as I have you, and I can paint—well, that's all the good luck I need.

About my shoulder. Did you know that when you touched me, I thought—Well, are you still sure this waiting stuff is the best thing? Guess I can wait another month. But that's all girl.

I love you,
Will.

THE JOURNAL:

How fitting, dear little old book, that you should end with my marriage, the happiness for which I've so longed. You have been a good counselor and confidante. You told Will more than he might have learned for some time. Our wedding was a dream come true. His family, mine, and all our friends were there. Both Elroy and Royal walked me down the little aisle, and Katherine was my Witness. I wore a real veil like they do back East with flowers from Aunt Stella's garden to hold it in place. We had punch and cookies back at the house with all my wonderful gifts laid out around the hope chest. Aunt Stella made her famous fruit-cake and it looked so lovely with pale pink icing on it that just matched the roses. So—Thus ends my life record thus far, on the very last page. I will begin anew in another little book as I record OUR life together. Oh, yes. Just between you and me, it was worth the wait.

The following was written by Thomas Carrol Schrack of Denver Colorado, and describes the homestead and early years of his parents who were part of the inspiration for THE HOPE CHEST. Tom was born in the very shack that is described by Eva Jean's, Thomas.

A FARM OF THEIR OWN

My parents, Vern and Mabel Schrack, arrived at the Homestead in January 1918. They had been married Christmas Day, 1917 at Mabel's family home in Clarinda, Iowa, an exciting and happy time for two young people in love. Their dream was to have a farm of their own, and they could perceive only a future filled with promise. Awaiting them was a small tarpaper shack built by Vern in the fall of 1917. It was located one mile north of the east end of the Hogbacks, six and one-half miles northeast of Stoneham, Weld County, Colorado. Dwarfed by the vastness of the prairie, the modest little building could not have been very impressive. This was mother's first look at the plot of land that would be her home for the next fifty-six years. She was familiar only with the verdant landscape of southwestern Iowa and when the euphoria of this new adventure was tempered with reality, there must have been some homesickness and disappointment. This experience would not have been unique to Mother. It was shared by thousands of homestead wives.

I recall reading years ago, a beautiful tribute to pioneering women, written by an unknown author.

"When the bride stepped out of the wagon, and her dainty feet touched the ground, the wilderness became a home."

The first years on the homestead were busy. A well had to be dug, sheds and corrals were necessary, milk cows and chickens had to be purchased and tended.

171

My parents returned to Clarinda, Iowa in the fall of 1918 in anticipation of the birth of their first child, Lila Hazel Schrack who was born on November 19, 1918.

Sometime after this event the original shack was enlarged to about twice its size by extending it lengthwise to the north; a substantial structure built with the help of a neighbor, Robert Huff. This was painted white and adjoined the shack to the south. Pictures remind you of a toy wooden train with an oversize engine heading south.

My sister Mary Ellen was born December 20, 1920, again in Clarinda. I was born on January 12, 1923, the only child born on the Homestead.

Although the first years were difficult, they were also encouraging. Each year more sod was being broken and planted to wheat and barley. Increased grain production created a business opportunity for Dad. Consequently, he purchased a used threshing machine and tractor and began threshing for hire in 1919. The business flourished for the next several years.

Mother had a responsibility of managing the household and farm chores alone for many weeks each fall. The only contact she had with the outside world was a rural mail carrier, who daily delivered mail and a day old newspaper. No radio, no telephone, no car, no contact with neighbors for days at a time, she lived day after day with endless chores and worry.

The year 1926 brought more improved housing. The white kitchen was moved east and incorporated into a new four-room, two-story building. It became a three-gabled house with two screened—in porches. Mother had a new house, 5 rooms with a full basement. The house remained as built, until extensive remodeling in the 1950's.

Brother Duane was born in October of 1926 in Sterling. By then a "Delco" 32 volt light plant was installed in the basement. In addition to electric lights, Mother now had many small kitchen appliances.

Rolland Lee was born in November of 1929, also in Sterling. Severe winter storms kept Mother in Sterling for three weeks.

She was then able to get to Stoneham on the "Prairie Dog Special" where she was met by a horse drawn sled for the ride to the Homestead where we eagerly awaited our new baby brother.

The depression and drought, together seemed an unfair burden for dry land farmers. Looking back, I'm sure our parents teetered on the brink of despair many times. For years a malaise hung over the country and would not go away. Income from threshing dwindled considerably and we survived by milking many cows, selling the cream and feeding the skim milk to the pigs. Change did come, and the last few years of the 30's brought some renewed optimism and hope.

We were to lose Rolland in the spring of 1941 when Dad was away from home. He was rushed to Sterling with a ruptured appendix. He died the same day that Uncle Royal's daughter Carole was born, far away in Buffalo, New York. It was a terrible time for us all.

The war years brought rapid changes to our community. Cattle and wheat prices rose. Many original Homesteaders had reached retirement age and left. New people and new methods took over. The days of the threshing machine and its crews were numbered. The combine, which cut and threshed in one operation, was now the universally accepted way to harvest. Thus passed another important part of prairie life. Threshing was a social time, an opportunity for fellowship with neighbors, reminiscent of the threshing bees and husking bees of early America. Hard, monotonous work is easier if you have company.

No small part of threshing was the contribution required of women. Three bountiful meals a day could always be anticipated. There was no modern plumbing, water was pumped and carried inside in a bucket. Their work started probably at 5:00am, and continued until the last of the supper dishes were washed. Threshing crews normally would number from 10-20 people. No wonder the women coined the phrase, "We are glad to see the threshers come but gladder yet to see them go."

The old Case thresher rolled home to its parking place west of the granary in 1950. It was moved near Stoneham, on Highway

14 by relatives of Vern Schrack. It sits there still on display, an abandoned relic, a reminder of a time that was.

The prairie has many moods: howling blizzards rage out of the northwest like a world gone mad, to ravage anything alive that hasn't found shelter, hot summer winds wither crops and torment people, early spring dust storms destroy crops and rob the land of topsoil. But what we remember most are beautiful spring days; refreshing rain and lush buffalo grass that fattens horses and calves; the smell of new plowed earth and the song of the meadowlark—the eternal hope that comes with each spring. This year will be better!

Those who stayed on the prairie tolerated its capricious nature. They realized its shortcomings and learned to respect its potential. Original homesteads were not a viable production unit. They had to be expanded. People who came to terms with their land were successful. This unique place in northeastern Colorado became a cherished home to my parents and scores of other families.

A granddaughter of Vern and Mabel Schrack, Kay Willich Dollerschell, and her husband Gary, became owners of the Schrack Homestead in 1973. The original shack still stands, a reminder to children, grandchildren and great grandchildren of the legacy we share from two young people who, long ago, made a commitment to "have a farm of their own."

Early 1900's. The way they were.

The actual shack, built in 1917 in Stoneham Co. with its owner, Vern Schrack, that was the model for Thomas' and Thea's home in Stoneham Co.

Tom C. Schrack. The model for Little Willie.

Lila Schrack, schoolmarm, Vim, CO. 1938. Married in 1939,
she was not allowed to continue teaching.